"I'll not have you calling me Your Highness in bed.

Call me Gabriel."

"Gabriel," she echoed, her soft voice low and intimate in a way that warmed his blood. "I promise to remember never to refer to you as Your Royal Highness or Prince Gabriel while we are making love."

Away from the public eye, Olivia was no longer the enigmatic, cultured woman he'd decided to marry. Impish humor sparkled in her eyes. Intelligence shone there, as well. Why had she hidden her sharp mind from him?

"All of a sudden, it occurs to me that I've never kissed you."

"You kissed me the day you proposed."

"In front of a dozen witnesses," he murmured. It had been a formality, really, not a true proposal. "And not the way I wanted to."

"How did you want to?"

"Like this."

* * *

Royal Heirs Re

Harlequin Desire's #1 bestselling series,
Billionaires and Babies: Powerful men...wrapped around their babies' little fingers.

* * *

If you're on Twitter,
tell us what you think of Harlequin Desire!
#harlequindesire

Dear Reader,

Royal Heirs Required begins a three-book series set in the imaginary kingdom of Sherdana, a landlocked country between France and Italy. Inspiration for the trio of stories came from *The Princess Diaries* movies, my love of Regency-set romances and a visit to the Greek Ionian Islands.

Since this is my first venture into Europe and royalty, I spent a fair amount of time online, researching palace interiors, couture fashion and all things weddings. About halfway through the book I discovered a little something called Pinterest and a new obsession was born.

Because pictures help me create the atmosphere in my stories, I appreciated having the ability to Pin photos for items and places that appear in my book. In fact, this worked so well that I've decided each book will have its own Pinterest board so readers can see what sparks my imagination.

I hope you enjoy spending time with Olivia and Gabriel. If you want to check out the Pinterest board for *Royal Heirs Required*, you can find it here: pinterest.com/catschieldbooks/hd-royal-heirs-required/.

All the best,

Cat Schield

ROYAL HEIRS REQUIRED

———

CAT SCHIELD

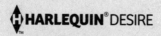

Recycling programs
for this product may
not exist in your area.

ISBN-13: 978-0-373-73372-9

Royal Heirs Required

Copyright © 2015 by Catherine Schield

HARLEQUIN®
www.Harlequin.com

Printed in U.S.A.

Cat Schield has been reading and writing romance since high school. Although she graduated from college with a BA in business, her idea of a perfect career was writing books for Harlequin. And now, after winning the Romance Writers of America 2010 Golden Heart® Award for series contemporary romance, that dream has come true. Cat lives in Minnesota with her daughter, Emily, and their Burmese cat. When she's not writing sexy, romantic stories for Harlequin Desire, she can be found sailing with friends on the St. Croix River, or in more exotic locales, like the Caribbean and Europe. She loves to hear from readers. Find her at catschield.com. Follow her on Twitter: @catschield.

Books by Cat Schield

HARLEQUIN DESIRE

Las Vegas Nights

At Odds with the Heiress
A Merger by Marriage
A Taste of Temptation

The Sherdana Royals

Royal Heirs Required

Visit the Author Profile page
at Harlequin.com for more titles.

For Delores and Jerry Slawik. Thank you for
making me feel like part of your family.

One

"She's the perfect choice for you," Gabriel Alessandro's brother joked, nudging his shoulder.

The two princes were standing at the edge of the dance floor watching their father, the king, sweep Gabriel's future bride through a series of elegant turns while their mother concentrated on keeping her toes from beneath the prime minister's clumsy feet.

Gabriel released an audible sigh. With his future bride's father building a high-tech manufacturing plant just outside the capital, Sherdana's economy would receive the boost it badly needed. "Of course she is."

Lady Olivia Darcy, daughter of a wealthy British earl, was just a little too perfect. While she exuded poise and warmth in public, in private she never relaxed, never let down her guard. This hadn't bothered him at all in the days leading up to their engagement. From the moment he'd begun looking for a wife he'd decided to listen to his head and not his heart. Past experience had demonstrated losing himself in passion led to nothing but heartache and disappointment.

"Then why are you looking so grim?"

Why indeed? Even though Gabriel didn't have to pretend to be besotted with his fiancée in front of his brother, he wasn't about to admit his regret that his personal life would have less passion and drama once he was married.

Until the wedding planning had begun in earnest, he'd considered himself well and thoroughly lucky to have found a woman who wouldn't drive him mad with her theatrics and demands. It was in sharp contrast to his affair with Marissa, which had been a tempestuous four-year romance with no future.

Gabriel was not a world-famous musician or a dashing Hollywood actor or even a wealthy playboy. He was the heir apparent of a small European country with strict laws that dictated his wife must be either an aristocrat or a citizen of Sherdana. Marissa had been neither.

"How happy would you be if you were marrying a virtual stranger?" Gabriel kept his voice soft, but there was no hiding his bitterness.

Christian's grin was positively wicked. "The best part about being the youngest is that I don't have to worry about getting married at all."

Gabriel muttered an expletive. He was well aware that neither of his brothers envied him. In many ways that was a relief. In centuries past Sherdana had seen its fair share of plots against the crown both from without and within. It would have been awful if either of his brothers had schemed to keep him off the throne. But that was highly unlikely. Nic lived in the US, building rocket ships that might someday carry regular—wealthy—citizens into space while Christian was very happy buying and selling companies.

"...hot."

"Hot?" Gabriel caught the final word his brother had spoken. "What's hot?"

"Not what." Christian shot him a wry glance. "Who. Your future bride. I was just remarking that you should spend some time getting to know her. It might be more enjoyable than you think. She's hot."

Lady Olivia Darcy was many things, but Gabriel wouldn't label her as hot. A gorgeous package of stylish sophistication, she had the fashion designers competing to dress her. Her features were delicate and feminine, her skin pale and unblemished. She was slender, but not boy-ish, with long legs, graceful arms and an elegant neck. There was a serene expression in her keen blue gaze.

And it wasn't as if she was a frivolous socialite, spend-ing her days shopping and her nights in clubs. She worked tirelessly for almost a dozen charities all focused on chil-dren's causes. The perfect future queen of Sherdana.

Gabriel shot his brother a narrow look. "You just re-ferred to your future sister-in-law and queen as hot. Do you think Mother would approve?"

"I'm her baby boy." The youngest of the triplets, Chris-tian had played the birth-order card all his life. "She ap-proves of everything I do."

"She doesn't approve of your antics, she simply feels bad for all those times she had to leave you to the nanny because she could only carry Nic and me."

Ignoring his brother's gibe, Christian nodded toward the queen. "She's hot, too, you know. She'd have to be to keep Father interested all these years."

Gabriel had no interest in discussing his parents' love life. "What has you so determined to stir up trouble to-night?"

Christian's expression settled into severe lines. "Now that Mother has you all settled, she going to turn her sights to Nic and me."

"Nic is more interested in fuel systems than women," Gabriel said. "And you've made it clear you have no in-tention of giving up your bachelor ways."

In the five years since his car accident, Christian had become guarded and pessimistic when it came to his per-sonal life. Although the burn scars that spread down his neck and over his shoulder, chest and upper arm on the right side were hidden beneath the high collar of his formal blue tunic, the worst of Christian's hurts were below the skin, deep in his soul where no healing reached. The damage was visible in those rare moments when he drank too much or thought no one was watching.

Gabriel continued, "I don't think either of our parents hold out any hope that the two of you will settle down anytime soon."

"You know Mother is a romantic," Christian said.

"She's also pragmatic."

But Christian didn't look convinced. "If that was true, she'd accept that you will father all the heirs Sherdana could ever want or need and leave Nic and me alone. That's not the impression she gave me earlier this evening."

A knot of discomfort formed in Gabriel's chest as he thought of his future bride. Once again his gaze slid to Olivia, who was now dancing with the prime minister. Although her smile was lovely, the reserve in her blue eyes made her seem untouchable.

His days with Marissa had been sensual, wild and all-consuming. They'd awaken before dawn in her Paris apartment and make love in the quiet hush of the early morning. After which they'd sit by the window, gorge themselves with pastries washed down with strong coffee and watch the sun paint the rooftops with golden light.

"Your Royal Highness."

Gabriel turned to his private secretary, who'd appeared out of nowhere. Usually Stewart Barnes was the calm eye in the middle of the hurricane. At the moment, sweat shone on his forehead.

The hairs on the back of Gabriel's neck rose. "Problem?"

Stewart's approach had caught Christian's attention, as well. "I'll deal with it," he said, stepping away from his brother's side.

"No, sir." The private secretary moved to block Christian. He gave a small shake of his head and met Gabriel's hard gaze with a look that conveyed the seriousness of the issue. "I know the timing is bad, but a lawyer has arrived with an urgent message for you."

"A lawyer?"

"How did he get into the palace?" Christian snapped, eyes blazing.

Gabriel barely registered Christian's words. "What could possibly be so important?"

"Did Captain Poulin give you a reason for granting this man entrance at such an inappropriate hour?"

"Can't it wait until after the party?"

Stewart's attention bounced between the two men as they fired questions at him. "He wouldn't tell me what it's about, Highness, only the name of his client." Stewart's tone was low and urgent. "I think you'd better speak to him."

Unable to imagine what could have rattled his unflappable private secretary, Gabriel shared a glance with Christian. "Who is his client?"

"Marissa Somme."

Hearing his former lover's name aroused a hundred emotions Gabriel would have preferred not to feel. He was a little surprised that Marissa had waited so long to contact him. He'd expected her to pull a stunt five months ago when he'd announced his engagement. To say she had a flare for the dramatic was like describing the Himalayas as tall hills.

"What mischief is she up to?" Gabriel demanded.

Christian cursed beneath his breath. "Something newsworthy, no doubt."

"I can't afford anything to interfere with the wedding." Sherdana's future was riding on the deal he'd struck with Lord Darcy. A deal that wouldn't be sealed until Olivia became a princess.

Gabriel glanced around to see if anyone had noticed their exchange and met Olivia's level gaze. She was beautiful, his future wife. But he'd chosen her for more than her appearance. She had a purity of spirit he knew would charm the Sherdanian people and her efficient, calm way of handling problems would see her through the hectic days ahead.

Beside her his father was laughing at whatever story she was telling him, looking years younger. Recent economic difficulties had taken their toll on the king. Once vibrant and strong, he'd begun to tire faster in recent months. It was why Gabriel had taken on more and more of the day-to-day running of the country.

Although she returned her attention to the king, the slightest lift of her delicate eyebrows let Gabriel know her curiosity had been aroused by his exchange with Christian and Stewart. Awareness surged through him. It was the first time that they'd connected at a level deeper than politeness. Anticipation sparked. Perhaps they would be able to share something more than a bed.

"Please, Your Highness."

Glancing toward Christian, he said, "Will you go entertain my fiancée while I discover what's going on?"

"Don't you mean distract?" Christian countered, his expression sour.

"Just make excuses for me until I can get back."

And then he was slipping through the multitude attending the ball honoring Sherdana's independence from France back in 1664, smiling and greeting the guests as if nothing in the world was wrong. All the while two words pounded in his head: *Marissa Somme.* What could this be about?

Since it first declared itself a principality, Sherdana had survived as an agrarian economy. But Gabriel wanted his country to do more than survive, he wanted it to thrive.

Tucked between France and Italy on a verdant plane re-splendent with grapevines and fertile fields, Sherdana needed an active technological culture to move the economy into the twenty-first century and beyond. Olivia's father, Lord Edwin Darcy, held the match that would light the fuse. Nothing must interfere with that.

Entering the green salon, Gabriel strode over to greet the man who'd barged in unannounced. The lawyer wore his gray hair short, making no attempt to hide the bald patch that caught the light from the wall sconces behind him. His clear gray eyes had few lines at the corners. This was not a man who smiled often. Dressed in a navy suit and black overcoat, the only spark of color about him was a thin line of yellow in his striped tie.

"Good evening, Your Royal Highness," the gentleman said, bowing respectfully. "Forgive me for interrupting, but I'm afraid the matter is quite urgent."

"What mischief is Marissa up to now?"

"Mischief?" The man looked dismayed at Gabriel's harshness. "You misunderstand the reason I'm here."

"Then enlighten me. I have guests waiting. If you have a message from Marissa, then deliver it."

The man straightened his shoulders and tugged at his coat lapel. "It's a little more complicated than a message."

"My patience is wearing thin."

"Marissa Somme is dead."

Dead? Gabriel felt as if he'd been clobbered with a poker. For a second he couldn't process the man's words. Brilliant, beautiful, vivacious Marissa dead? His gut twisted.

"How?"

The older gentleman nodded in sympathy. "Cancer."

Even though he hadn't spoken with her in a very long time, the news rocked him. Marissa had been the first woman he'd ever loved. The only one. Their breakup three years before had been one of the most painful experiences of his life. But nothing compared to knowing she was gone for good. Wounds he'd thought healed were reopened, the pain as fresh as it had ever been. Never would he see her again. Hear her laugh.

Why hadn't she called him? He would have helped her out.

"You came all this way to deliver the news of her death to me?" Had she still cared about him? Despite her final angry words? Impossible. She'd never once tried to contact him.

"And to bring you something she said you should have."

"What?" Gabriel demanded. Had she returned the diamond heart pendant he'd given her for their first anniversary? He'd been a romantic fool in those days. Young. Rebellious. Caught up in a passionate affair that had no future. And a fool. "What did you bring me?"

"Your daughters."

"Daughters?" *As in more than one?* Gabriel wondered if he'd heard the man properly.

"Twins."

"Marissa and I had no children together."

"I'm afraid that's not true."

The man pulled out two birth certificates and extended them. Gabriel gestured to Stewart to take them and watched as his private secretary scanned the documents. Stewart's blue eyes were awash with concern as he glanced up and met Gabriel's gaze.

"They bear Marissa's last name, but she listed you as the father," Stewart said.

"They can't be mine," Gabriel insisted. "We were careful." Perhaps not careful enough. "How old are they?"

"They will turn two in a month."

Gabriel quickly did the math. They'd been conceived in the week he'd been in Venice shortly after their breakup.

Marissa had come and thrown herself at him in one last attempt to make him abandon his duty. They'd made love all night, their kisses frantic, embraces feverish. When she'd awakened to find him departing the room before dawn, she'd lashed out, claiming that he'd led her on, accusing him of indifference. Despite her antagonism, regret had stuck with him for months afterward.

They'd had no future. His duty was to his country. She couldn't accept that and he'd let the relationship go on too long. She'd begun to hope he would give up everything for her and he'd enjoyed shirking his responsibilities. But it couldn't last. Sherdana always came first.

What would he have done if he'd known she was pregnant? Set her up in a villa nearby where he could visit? She would never have put up with that. She'd have demanded his complete and total devotion. It was what had torn them apart. He belonged to the people of Sherdana.

"This could all be a huge hoax," Stewart said.

"Marissa might have loved drama, but pulling a stunt like this goes beyond anything she'd do."

"We'll know for sure after a DNA test," Stewart said.

"And in the meantime? What am I to do with the girls?" the lawyer asked impertinently.

"Where are they?" Gabriel demanded. He crackled with impatience to see them.

"Back at my hotel with their nanny."

He didn't hesitate to ponder the consequences. "Get them."

"Think of your upcoming wedding, Highness," Stewart cautioned. "You can't have them brought here. The palace is crawling with media."

Gabriel aimed a disgusted look at his secretary. "Are you telling me you're not clever enough to transport two toddlers here without being seen?"

Stewart's spine snapped straight as Gabriel knew it

would. "I will see that they are brought to the palace immediately."

"Good."

"In the meantime," Stewart said, "I suggest you return to the gala before you're missed. I'm sure the king and queen will wish to discuss the best way to handle things."

Gabriel hated every bit of Stewart's sensible advice and the need to play host when his attention was shackled to reckless urges. He didn't want to wait to see the girls. His instinct demanded he go to the lawyer's hotel immediately. As if by taking one look at the toddlers he could tell if they were his. Ridiculous.

"Find me as soon as they're settled," he told Stewart.

And with those parting words, he exited the room.

Knowing he should return immediately to the party but with his mind racing, Gabriel strode into the library. He needed a few minutes to catch his breath and calm his thoughts.

Twins. His heart jerked. Did they have their mother's clear green eyes and luxurious brown hair? Had she told them about him? Was he insane to bring them into the palace?

A scandal could jeopardize his plans for stabilizing Sherdana's economy. Would the earl still allow Olivia to marry him if word got out that Gabriel had illegitimate twin daughters? And what if Olivia wasn't willing to accept that her children wouldn't be his only ones?

Gabriel left the library, burdened by a whole new set of worries, determined to make sure his future bride found him irresistible.

From her place of honor beside the king of Sherdana, Olivia watched her future husband slip through the guests assembled in the golden ballroom and wondered what was so important that he had to leave the Independence Day gala in such a hurry.

It continued to bother her that in less than four weeks, she was going to become a princess, Gabriel's princess, and she had very little insight into the man she was marrying. Theirs was not a love match the likes of which Kate had found with William. Olivia and Gabriel were marrying to raise her father's social position and improve Sherdana's economic situation.

While that was great for everyone else, Olivia's London friends wondered what was motivating her. She'd never told anyone about the dream conceived by her three-year-old self that one day she'd become a princess. It had been a child's fancy and as she'd grown up, reality replaced the fairy tale. As a teenager she'd stopped imagining herself living in a palace and dancing through the night with a handsome prince. Her plans for the future involved practical things like children's charities and someday a husband and children of her own. But some dreams had deep roots that lay dormant until the time was ripe.

Before Olivia considered her actions, she turned to the king. "Excuse me."

"Of course," the handsome monarch replied, his smile cordial.

Released, she left the king and headed in the direction her fiancé had gone. Perhaps she could catch Gabriel before he returned to the ballroom and they could spend some time talking, just the two of them. She hadn't gone more than a dozen steps before Christian Alessandro appeared in her path.

His gold eyes, shadowed and wary around most people, warmed as he smiled down at her. "Are you enjoying the party?"

"Of course," she replied, bottling up a sigh as the youngest Alessandro prince foiled her plan to speak to his brother alone.

She'd encountered Christian several times in London over the years. As the wildest Alessandro brother, in his university days, Christian had spent more time partying than studying and had barely graduated from Oxford. He'd earned a reputation as a playboy, but had always treated her with respect. Maybe because Olivia had recognized the clever mind he hid beneath his cavalier charm.

"I noticed Prince Gabriel left the party in a hurry," she murmured, unable to conquer the curiosity that loosened her tongue. "I hope nothing is wrong."

Christian had an impressive poker face. "Just some old business he had to take care of. Nothing important."

"He looked a bit shaken up." She stared at her future brother-in-law and saw the tiniest twitch at the corner of his eye. He was keeping something important about Gabriel from her. Olivia's pulse skipped. Seemed she wasn't the only one with secrets.

Since Gabriel had opened negotiations with her father a year ago, Olivia hadn't had much opportunity to get to know the man she would marry. The situation hadn't improved since she'd arrived in Sherdana a week ago. With the wedding only a month away and parliament in session, they'd barely spent an hour alone together and most of that had been divided up into one- to five-minute snippets.

A stroll in the garden the day after she'd arrived, cut short when they'd met the queen's very muddy vizsla. Gabriel had commended Olivia's nimbleness in dodging the dog and retreated to the palace to change his trousers.

A moment in the carriage before the parade yesterday. He'd complimented her hat.

A whole five minutes during the waltz this evening. He'd told her she looked lovely.

Their exchanges were polite and cordial. At all times

he'd been the perfect prince. Courteous. Gallant. Cultured. And she'd been seized by the absurd desire to muss his hair and shock him with outrageous remarks. Of course, she would never do that. The daughter of an earl, she was acutely conscious of her image and position.

Christian refocused her attention on the crowd around them and began filling her ear with all sorts of salacious gossip about the local nobility. Normally she'd be amused by his outrageous slander of Sherdana's wealthy and powerful, but with each new dance the air in the ballroom grew stuffier and she wanted to spend time getting to know her fiancé.

What did Gabriel expect from her? A political partner? Or an attractive figurehead that he could trot out for state occasions? She hoped it was the former.

Firstborn, he'd won the right to inherit the throne by a mere forty minutes. But there was no question in anyone's mind that he was utterly and completely suited to the role.

His commitment to Sherdana was absolute and apparent to all. He'd been educated here and rarely left, except on official business. While in contrast, his two younger brothers had both chosen to spend as little time in their native country as possible.

Drawn by a magnetic pull too great to resist, her attention returned to the ballroom doors that Gabriel had passed through. What could have taken him away in the middle of the party? As if her thoughts had summoned him, she spied the prince coming through the crowd toward her.

Her gaze traced the sculpted breadth of his shoulders, the way his white jacket stretched across his broad chest, providing an abundance of room for the medals pinned there. A blue sash cut diagonally from shoulder to hip.

"Forgive me for neglecting you," he said as he came to a stop before her. "I hope my brother has kept you sufficiently entertained."

"Christian has been filling me in on your guests."

For the first time in her company, Gabriel's courteous mask slipped. He shot his brother a hard look. "What have you been telling her?"

"Things most people, including you, wouldn't. If she's going to be Sherdana's princess, she needs to know where the bodies are buried or she'll be no help to you at all."

Gabriel shook his head. "She doesn't need to know all the ins and outs of our politics to help out the country or me."

Olivia's heart sank. Now she knew what he expected from her. There would be no partnership, no working together. She would attend ceremonies and support charities while he ran the country and dealt with its problems alone.

"She's smarter than you're giving her credit for, Gabriel. You should use her to your best political advantage."

"Thank you for your opinion, brother." And his tone said that was the end of the conversation.

With a mocking bow, Christian retreated. While part of Olivia regretted his departure, she was glad for a moment alone with Gabriel. Or she was until he began to speak.

"I know you haven't seen much of Sherdana since your arrival," he said, his polite formality pushing her to greater impatience. "But maybe that can change in the next week or so."

"That would be lovely." She bit back her thoughts on how unlikely it was. With the wedding only a month away she would scarcely have the opportunity to sleep, much less take a tour of the countryside. "I'm eager to visit the wine country."

"Sherdana takes pride in its wine as you well know."

"As it should," she murmured, her boredom coming through in her tone. "I'm glad you were able to get your business resolved so you could return to the party so quickly."

"Business?" There wasn't the least suggestion of understanding in his manner.

"I saw your private secretary approach you with some news. It seemed to be something unpleasant. And then you left. Christian explained it was old business you needed to take care of."

"Ah, yes. Just a misunderstanding with Stewart. It was nothing."

"I'm glad." But her mind was busy cataloging all the nuances of his tone and expression. Her future husband was skilled at deflection.

"Would you care to dance?" he asked, his deep voice rumbling through her like distant thunder.

Not really. She was tired and her shoes pinched. But she smiled. "Of course."

A waltz began to play as Gabriel took her hand and led her onto the dance floor. Keeping her expression pleasant and neutral was torture as his palm slid against her back. The gown she wore had a modest cut, showing no cleavage or bare shoulders, but the material was silk and the heat of Gabriel's hand burned through the fabric and set her on fire.

"Are you feeling compelled to marry because your father wishes it?"

The abruptness of his question was so unexpected, she almost laughed. "Why would I need to be compelled by my father? You're rich, handsome and going to be king one day. What girl wouldn't wish to be queen?"

"You didn't answer my question."

"I'm not being forced to marry you. I have been given an opportunity many would envy." She assessed his expression, curious where this line of questioning originated. "Are you worried that down the road I'll regret my choice?" She cocked her head and regarded him intently. "Or are you looking for an excuse to break our engagement?"

"Nothing like that. I am just wondering if perhaps you'd have preferred a different life."

"I'm sure many people wish every day that they'd done something different. Mostly, we must play the hand life deals us. For some, it's struggling with poverty. For others raising a child on their own or dedicating themselves to their career and forgoing a family." She pitched her voice into sympathetic tones for the next example. "For you it's ensuring your kingdom's economic security. I get to marry a prince and someday become a queen."

For some inexplicable reason, he grew short with her. "But is that what you want?"

"To marry you and become a queen?" She let her surprise show. "Of course."

Gabriel didn't appear convinced. "We haven't had much time to get to know each other," he said. "I hope that will change over the next month."

"Perhaps we could begin now. What is it you'd like to know?"

"Let's begin simply. How do you come to speak French and Italian so fluently?"

"I had a whole army of tutors from the time I was small."

"Your accent is quite good."

"I've been told I have an aptitude for languages. I speak quite a few."

"How many?"

"Six, but I understand three more."

"That will come in handy when dignitaries visit us."

Once again it hit her that she would never return to her home in England for anything more than a short visit. As princess, she would be expected to spend most, if not all, of her time in Sherdana. At least she would see her father frequently because he would want to keep an eye on his investment.

"You don't smile much, do you?" His question was more reflective than directly aimed at her.

His observation caught her off guard.

"I smile all the time."

Gabriel's gaze slipped intently over her features, arousing a frantic thrumming in her chest. "Polite smiles. Political smiles, but I'm not sure I've once seen you smile because you're happy."

"I assure you, I'm quite happy."

"Stop telling me what you think I want to hear. That's not what Sherdana needs of its princess and definitely not what I expect from my wife."

The intensity of his tone and the nuances of his observation did not belong to the man she'd known up to this point. His frank speech loosened her tongue.

"Are you giving me permission to argue with Your Highness?"

He made a face. "Gabriel."

"Of course."

"Olivia." Tone commanding, he somehow managed to caress her name in a way that vibrated through her. "It would make me very happy if you would start thinking of me as a man and not a prince."

His demand sent a ripple of excitement up her spine. She decided to speak her mind.

"I will if you stop thinking of me in terms of economic gain or financial dealings and realize I'm a woman who knows exactly what she wants."

At her words, Gabriel blinked. Surprise quickly became curiosity as he regarded her. For the first time she believed he was seeing her as a person instead of the clause in the contract he needed to satisfy so her father would build a plant in Sherdana and create technical jobs to bolster the economy.

"I'm beginning to think there's more to you than I realize," Gabriel remarked, executing a turn in the dance that left her breathless.

"Thank goodness." It was an effort to get out more than those two words.

Perhaps marriage might hold more of an adventure than she'd first thought. She hadn't expected her husband to excite her. Even seeing how handsome Gabriel was, he was always so in control. She never imagined passion. And growing up sheltered from the experiences an ordinary girl would have with boys such as dating or even just hanging out, she'd never experienced desire. Until this moment, she wasn't sure she could.

Relief made her giddy. Tonight she'd glimpsed a very important and unexpected benefit this marriage would have for her and for the first time in months, she faced her future with a light heart.

Two

Olivia lay on the blue velvet chaise in the bedroom she'd been assigned at the palace, a heating pad taking away the discomfort of cramps. She stared up at the touches of gold leaf on the ceiling's ornate plasterwork twenty feet above her. From the tall, narrow mirrors between the wide cream silk-draped windows to the elegant chandeliers, it was a stunning, yet surprisingly warm, space.

It was a little after two in the morning. She'd felt the first twinge of pain not long after the king and queen left the gala and had taken the opportunity to slip away. The attack had been blessedly mild. A year ago, she would have taken a pain pill and retreated to bed. Thank goodness those days were behind her. A princess couldn't avoid public appearances because she wasn't feeling well. She must have a spine of steel and prove her value was more than the economic boost her father's new technology company would provide.

As if to mock her optimism, a fresh ache began. She'd first started suffering with sharp cramps and strong periods when she was fifteen. Frightened by the amount of blood she lost each month, Olivia had gone to see a doctor. She'd been diagnosed with endometriosis and had begun taking oral contraceptives to reduce the pain and shorten her periods. Yoga, massage and acupuncture had also helped her cope with her symptoms, but none of these could correct the problem.

She'd needed surgery for that.

Olivia couldn't explain why she'd been so reluctant to have the growths removed when the pain grew progressively worse in her early twenties. She couldn't share her fears with her mother—who'd died giving birth to her—so she'd hidden the severity of the problem from everyone, including her father. Only Libby, her private secretary, knew how debilitating the pain could get. Libby had helped Olivia keep her doctor visits out of the press and made excuses when she had bad days. Olivia wasn't sure what she'd have done these past eight years without Libby's help.

It wasn't until a year ago, when she'd confronted the connection between endometriosis and infertility, that she began to rethink her plans for coping with the disease. If she was marrying a wealthy businessman, a politician or even one of her own country's nobles, she could discuss this issue with him and together they could decide what to do about her potential barrenness. But she was marrying the future king of Sherdana and would be expected to produce an heir.

So, she'd had the surgery and had been living pain free for almost twelve months.

With a sudden surge of impatience, Olivia set aside the heating pad and got to her feet. Brooding over her medical condition was the quickest way to doubt herself and that wasn't the way she faced things. Despite the late hour, the luxurious king-size bed held no appeal. She needed some fresh air and exercise. Perhaps a walk in the garden.

Although she'd removed her ball gown upon returning to her room, she'd not yet dressed for bed. Slipping off her robe, Olivia pulled on a sleeveless jersey dress and found a pair of ballet flats that would allow her to move soundlessly through the sleeping palace.

The room she'd been given was in the opposite wing of the palace from the royal family's apartments and used for housing dignitaries and visitors. Her father slept next door, his room as expansive and substantially furnished as hers. Olivia tiptoed past his door, aiming for the stairs at the far end of the hall that would deposit her close to the pink receiving room and the side gardens beyond. With her limited time in the palace, Olivia hadn't had a great deal of time to explore, but she'd taken this route her second day to meet with the queen.

When she got to the end of the hallway, the high-pitched shriek of an unhappy child caught Olivia's attention. The sound was muffled and it came from somewhere above her. She reached the stairs and paused to listen. She waited no more than a heartbeat before the cry came again, only this time there were two voices.

In an instant Olivia's destination changed. Instead of going down to the ground level, she headed up to the third floor, following the increasingly frantic exclamations of the children and the no less agitated voice of an adult trying to quiet them.

At the top of the stairs, Olivia spied two shadows racing toward her down the darkened hallway. Curious as to what was going on, she'd taken several steps in their direction when a voice cut through the shadows.

"Karina. Bethany. Come back here this instant." The shrill command provoked the children to faster flight.

Worried that at the speed they were going, they might pitch down the stairs, Olivia knelt and spread her arms wide. With their path blocked, the children stopped abruptly. With eyes wide, arms around each other for comfort, they stared at Olivia.

"Hello." She offered them her gentlest smile. "Where are you two going so late?"

"You girls are nothing but trouble."

The scolding woman hadn't spied Olivia in the dimness or she wouldn't have spoken so rudely. The two little girls shrank away from their pursuer, obviously afraid, and sidestepped in Olivia's direction. Now that they were closer, Olivia could see them better. She blinked, wondering if she might be seeing double.

The two little girls, two frightened little girls, were mirror images of each other with long brown hair and large dark eyes in their pale faces. They were dressed in identical dresses and tears streaked their matching cheeks.

Olivia wanted to snatch them into her arms, but feared upsetting them still more. Although her childhood had lacked a loving mother, Olivia had developed a strong maternal instinct. Being warned by the doctor that unless she had surgery she might never have her own children had been a sharp knife in her heart.

"You'd better learn to behave and fast or the people who live here will kick you out and you'll have nowhere else to go."

Having heard enough, Olivia surged to her feet to confront the woman and was surprised when the girls raced to stand behind her. They gripped her dress with strength born of fear, and protectiveness surged through her.

"Stop speaking this instant," Olivia commanded without raising her voice. "No one deserves to be threatened like that, especially not children."

The nanny stopped dead in her tracks and sneered. "You don't know what they're like."

"Whom do you work for?"

The woman looked wary. "I take care of these two."

"Yes, yes." Olivia put one hand on each of the toddlers' heads. The hair was silky beneath her fingers and she longed to give the girls her full attention, but this woman must be dealt with first. "But who are their parents?"

"Their mother is dead."

Olivia sucked in a short breath at the woman's lack of compassion. "That's awful."

The woman didn't respond.

"In heaven," the child on her left said.

Olivia liked the girls' nanny less and less. Had the woman no heart? Did the father know how badly his daughters were being cared for? "Perhaps I should speak to their father. What is his name?"

"A lawyer hired me a week ago to take care of them." The woman stared at Olivia in hostile defensiveness.

"Well, you're not doing a very good job."

"They're terribly spoiled and very difficult. And right now they need to be in bed." Eyes on the children, the nanny shifted her weight forward and her arms left her sides as if she intended to snatch the little girls away from Olivia.

The little girl on her right shrank back. Her sister, emboldened by Olivia's defense, fought back.

"Hate you." She hung on Olivia's skirt. "Wanna go home."

Although she'd been too young to know the shock of losing her mother, Olivia remembered her lonely childhood and ached for the sadness yet to come for these girls. She wanted to wrap her arms around the toddlers and support them through this difficult time, but these were not her children and she shouldn't get attached.

With a heavy sigh, Olivia knew it was time to extricate herself from the situation. She would summon a maid to get the girls settled and return to her room. In the morning she would find out to whom they belonged and fill him in on his employee.

"If I make this mean lady go away," Olivia began, gazing down at the dark heads. "Would you go back to your room and go to sleep?"

"No." Only one of the pair seemed to be verbal. The

other merely gave her head a vehement shake. "Stay with you."

Oh, dear. Obviously she'd defended the girls a little too well. But maybe it wouldn't hurt for them to spend one night with her. There was plenty of room in her big bed and in the morning she could sort them out.

"Would you like to come to my room to sleep tonight?"

In unison, the two dark heads bobbed. Olivia smiled.

"You can't do this," the nanny protested.

"I most certainly can. I suggest you return to your room and pack. I will send someone to escort you out shortly." Olivia extended a hand to each girl and drew the children toward the stairs. Once they were settled in her room, she would send a maid up for their nightgowns and things.

It took time to descend to the second floor. The toddlers' short legs made slow work of the steps, giving Olivia time to wonder who in the palace would raise a cry that they'd gone missing. She looked forward to having a conversation with their father in the near future about the sort of person he'd employed to take care of his children.

When Olivia entered her room, she was surprised to find it occupied by a maid. The girl looked up in surprise from the desk items she was straightening as the trio entered. Although the palace had provided Olivia with maids to tidy up and assist with whatever she needed, she hadn't expected to find one in her room during the middle of the night. And from the expression on the woman's face, she wasn't expecting to be caught at it.

"Lady Darcy, I was just tidying some things up for you."

"At two in the morning?"

"I saw your light on and thought you might be needing something."

Not wanting to make a huge scene in front of the little girls, Olivia scanned the maid's face, confident she'd be able to recognize her again from the hundred or so servants that maintained the palace. She had a small scar just below her left eye.

"Could you run down to the kitchen and get glasses of warm milk for these two?"

"Hate milk," the talkative one said. "Ice cream."

Recalling the nanny's assessment that the girls were spoiled, Olivia hesitated a moment before giving a mental shrug. Again she reminded herself they weren't her responsibility. She could indulge them to her heart's content. "With chocolate sauce?"

"Yeah!"

Olivia nodded. "Please fetch two bowls of ice cream with chocolate sauce."

"Of course, Lady Darcy."

The maid scooted past her, eyeing the odd group before disappearing through the doorway.

Olivia half sat, half collapsed on the sofa near the fireplace and gestured to the girls. "Let's get acquainted, shall we? My name is Olivia."

They hesitated for a moment before coming toward her. Olivia kept her warmest smile fixed on her face and patted the seat beside her.

"Please sit down. The ice cream will take a little while. The palace is very big."

The girls held hands and stared about the enormous room in wide-eyed silence. Now that she could see them better, Olivia noticed the Alessandro family resemblance. In fact, they looked like the pictures she'd seen of Gabriel's sister, Ariana, at a similar age. Were they cousins? She frowned. Her extensive research on Sherdana had included all the royal family. She recalled no mention of young cousins.

"I've only been here a few days and I've gotten lost a dozen times already," she continued, her voice a soothing monotone. "I was very scared when that happened. But I also discovered some wonderful places. There's a library downstairs full of books. Do you like stories?"

They nodded at her, their movements identical as if choreographed.

"So do I. My favorite stories when I was a little girl were about princesses. Would you like to hear one?" She took their smiles as assent. "Once upon a time there were two princesses and their names were Karina and Bethany."

"That's us."

Gabriel paced his office, impatient for Stewart to arrive with news that the twins had been settled into the palace. In his hand was the single photo he'd kept of Marissa after they'd broken up. He'd sealed it in an envelope and shoved it in the back of a drawer. Why he'd kept it was a question he was brooding over now.

After a long, unproductive strategy session with Christian regarding Marissa's daughters, he'd sent his brother home. Although he had rooms for his use in the palace, Christian liked his privacy and only rarely stayed in them. Sometimes Gabriel suspected that if either of his brothers had a choice they would give up their titles and any claim to Sherdana's throne. As it was they spent almost no time in Sherdana. Nic had gone to university in the US where he'd met his business partner and only returned when he absolutely had to, while Christian spent most of the year out of the country pursuing his business interests.

As close as the triplets had been growing up, the distance between them these days bothered Gabriel. While he'd known, as eldest son, that he'd be in charge of running the country someday, he'd never expected that his brothers wouldn't be around to help.

Stewart appeared as Gabriel was returning Marissa's photo to the envelope. Glancing at the clock he saw it was almost three in the morning. He'd sent his private secretary to check on Marissa's daughters half an hour earlier.

"Well?" he demanded, pushing to his feet.

"They arrived at the palace a couple hours ago and I arranged to have them escorted to the nursery in the north wing." It had seemed prudent to squirrel them away at the opposite end of the palace, far from where the royal family was housed.

"Have you seen them?" He wanted to know if the girls bore any resemblance to him, and could scarcely restrain himself from asking the question outright. Christian had cautioned that a DNA test would have to be performed before Gabriel let himself get emotionally involved. It was good advice, but easier agreed to than acted upon.

"Not yet."

Gabriel's temper flared. "What have you been doing?"

The private secretary wasn't fazed by his employer's impatience. "I went to the nursery, but they appear to be missing."

"Missing?" He couldn't imagine how that had happened. "Didn't the lawyer say they had a nanny? Did you ask her where they are?"

"She's gone. Apparently she was escorted from the palace by one of the guards an hour ago."

"Escorted…? On whose authority?"

"Lady Darcy's private secretary."

Unable to fathom how she'd gotten involved, Gabriel stabbed his fingers through his hair. This business with Marissa's daughters was fast spiraling out of control. "Have you spoken with her?"

"It's three in the morning, sir."

And if two little girls weren't missing, he might be inclined to leave his questions until morning. "Tell her I want to speak to her."

"Right away."

His private secretary wasn't gone more than five minutes. "Apparently she's in Lady Darcy's room, sir." Stewart paused. "With the girls."

Dismay shouldered aside irritation as Gabriel headed for the wing that housed his future bride. An encounter between Olivia and Marissa's daughters was a problem he hadn't anticipated. No doubt she would have questions about them. She was proving more troublesome than he'd expected based on their limited interaction before he'd proposed. Christian had warned him there was more to Olivia than a pretty face and polished manners, but she'd done an excellent job keeping her agenda hidden. The question was why.

Gabriel knocked on the door of Olivia's suite, agitation adding sharpness to the blows. His summons was answered more quickly than he expected by a pretty woman in her early thirties, wearing a classic blue dress and a frown. Her eyes widened as she spied him standing in the hall.

"I'm here looking for two little girls who've gone missing from the nursery," Gabriel said, his tone courteous despite the urge to push past her. "I understand they are here. May I come in?"

"Of course, Your Highness." She stepped back and gestured him in. "Lady Darcy, Prince Gabriel is here to see you."

"If you'll excuse us," Gabriel said, gesturing her out before entering the dimly lit suite and closing the door behind him.

His gaze swept the room in search of his fiancée. He spied her by the fireplace. She looked serene in a simple cotton dress, her hair in the same updo she'd worn to the gala. So she hadn't yet gone to bed. This thought made his attention shift to the large bed where he spied a lump beneath the covers.

"Sorry for the late visit," he told her. "But two children have gone missing."

"Bethany and Karina."

She knew their names. What else had she found out?

"What are they doing here?" he asked the question more sharply than he'd intended and saw her eyes narrow.

"They each had a bowl of ice cream and fell asleep." Her sweet smile had a bit of an edge. "They were terrified of that horrible woman who'd been hired to look after them and refused to sleep in their own beds. So I brought them here."

"And plied them with ice cream?"

"Their mother just died a few days ago. Strangers tore them from the only home they'd ever known and brought them to this big, scary place. Do you have any idea how traumatic all that was for them?"

"The nursery is not scary."

"It was for them. And so was that awful woman who was taking care of them."

"Is that why you had her escorted out of the palace tonight?"

Olivia's eyes flashed. "I suppose you're going to tell me it wasn't my place to fire her, but she reminded me of the villain in every children's story I've ever read."

Her outrage was charming and Gabriel found his annoyance melting away. "How did you come to meet them?"

"I couldn't sleep so I thought I'd go for a walk. When I got to the stairs I could hear their cries and the nanny's scolding. They were running down the hall away from that woman and the things she said to them." Olivia's lips tightened. "I would like to speak to their father about her. First thing tomorrow morning if at all possible."

"The situation with them is a little complicated," Gabriel told her, his gaze once again drawn to the lump in the center of the mattress.

"Then explain it to me."

This was what Gabriel had been wrestling with all evening. What he was going to tell the world about Marissa's daughters was a small issue compared to how he would explain things to his parents and the woman he would soon marry.

"Some matters need to be cleared up first."

Olivia's hard stare searched his expression for a long silent moment before she spoke. "What sort of matters?"

He couldn't tell her that the girls were none of her business when she'd already taken their care upon herself. At the same time, he didn't want to claim the girls before the matter of their heritage was cleared up.

"Perhaps you're referring to a DNA test." She laughed at his surprise. "They look like your sister when she was young."

"They do?"

"Didn't you notice?"

"They only just arrived. I haven't seen them yet."

Heart thumping hard against his ribs, Gabriel moved toward the bed. Since finding out about the twins, he'd been impatient to see them, but abruptly his feet felt encased in concrete. Caught between dread and hope that the girls belonged to him, Gabriel stared down at matching faces, peaceful and so innocent in sleep.

The breath he'd taken lodged in his chest as recognition flared. Marissa hadn't lied. They were his. He traced each of the children's delicate cheeks with his finger and his muscles slackened as relief washed over him.

"They're yours, aren't they?" Olivia's voice swelled with emotion, but when he glanced at her, her expression was as serene as if they were discussing the weather. "I had hoped they belonged to Christian."

"I just learned about them tonight."

"Their mother never told you?" Olivia sighed. "And now she's dead."

"Things ended badly between us." He couldn't face Olivia with his emotions this raw, so he kept his gaze on his daughters. "I didn't know she was ill." For a moment he was consumed by despair. He pressed his lips into a tight line. Then, feeling her watching him, he settled his features into an impassive mask.

"You loved her."

He and Olivia had never spoken of love. Their marriage was about politics, not romance. But if she suspected he'd given away his heart to another woman, she might not be so happy.

"We were together a long time ago."

"Karina and Bethany aren't even two. It wasn't that long ago."

Despite her neutral tone, Gabriel suspected she wasn't thrilled to have his past thrown so fully in her face. If the truth about the twins got out the press would speculate and create drama and controversy where there was none. Olivia would become the unwitting victim of their desire for ratings.

"This has to remain a secret," he told her.

"Impossible. The minute you brought them to the palace you risked word getting out."

"Perhaps, but I'd like to postpone that as long as possible so we can strategize how we're going to control the damage."

"If you're worried about my father's reaction, don't be. He's committed to opening a plant here."

"And you?"

"They're two precious little girls. I'll support whatever decision you make, but I think you should proudly claim them as yours."

Her eyes were clear of hesitation or deceit. Did she

realize this would make her a stepmother to his former lover's children? Would another woman have been so understanding?

"I can't figure you out."

"Your Highness?"

"Gabriel," he growled, amused rather than annoyed. "I'll not have you calling me Your Highness in bed."

The underlying heat in his voice reached her. Her cheeks flared pink.

"Gabriel," she echoed, her soft voice low and intimate in a way that warmed his blood. "I promise to remember never to refer to you as Your Royal Highness, or Prince Gabriel, while we're making love."

For the first time he glimpsed the Olivia beneath the enigmatic, cultured woman he'd decided to marry. Impish humor sparkled in her eyes. Intelligence shone there, as well. Why had she hidden her sharp mind from him? Gabriel considered how little time they they'd spent together and shouldered the blame. If he'd gotten to know her better, he'd have seen the truth much sooner.

"All of a sudden, it occurs to me that I've never kissed you." He took her hand and dusted a kiss over her knuckles.

"You kissed me the day you proposed."

"In front of a dozen witnesses," he murmured. He had asked her to marry him in front of her father and close relations. It had been a formality, really, not a true proposal. "And not the way I wanted to."

"How did you want to?"

She'd never flirted with him before and he discovered he liked the challenge in her gaze. Anticipation lit up the room as he set his finger beneath her chin and tilted her head, bringing her lips to a perfect angle to align with his. He watched her long lashes drift downward.

Her breath caught as he stopped just shy of brushing Olivia's lips. The disturbed rush of air awakened his senses with fierce urgency. He longed to crush her against him and feast on her soft mouth. Instead, he concentrated on the scent of her, a delicious floral that reminded him of a spring evening when the roses were in full bloom, while he reined his urges back under control.

What was happening to him? Her body's tension communicated across the short distance between them, the trembling of her muscles, a siren call that demanded he claim her. He was a little startled how compelling that desire was.

Ever since they'd danced, he'd been preoccupied with investigating the chemistry that had sparked between them. He hadn't expected to find passion in his marriage. But now that the sexual chemistry had flared, he couldn't wait to explore her every sigh and moan.

From the start she'd intrigued him. Every time they shared the same room, she'd claimed and held his attention. But he'd chosen her because of what her father's investment could mean for Sherdana rather than for any emotional connection between them. And then tonight she'd revealed that her tranquil exterior camouflaged a quick mind and determined nature.

"This might not be the best place for our first kiss," he told her, his voice raw and husky. Body aching in protest, Gabriel stepped back.

"I understand." She glanced toward his sleeping daughters.

But he doubted that she did because he barely understood his own actions.

No woman before or after Marissa had made him feel like losing all control, and it was logical to assume that no one ever would. Earlier he'd thought of Olivia as cool and untouchable. He'd been very wrong.

This abrupt and overwhelming craving to make love to her long into the night until she lay sated in his arms wasn't part of the plan. He needed a woman who would grace his side in public and warm his bed at night.

The operative word being *warm*.

Not set it on fire.

"I think they should stay here tonight," Olivia murmured, her words wresting him back to the other complication in his life. "In the morning, we can get them settled upstairs." She must have seen a protest building because she shook her head. "They're staying put. They've been through enough for one night. I want to make certain someone familiar is with them when they wake."

Gabriel's eyebrows rose at her adamant tone. "And you're that someone familiar?"

"I fed them ice cream," Olivia said, her expression lightening. "They'll be glad to see a friendly face."

"You certainly have that." He glanced toward the sleeping girls. "And a very beautiful one, as well."

Three

Olivia didn't sleep well on the couch. But she wasn't sure she'd have slept any better in her bed alone. She kept running through her evening. Rescuing the twins, discovering they were Gabriel's illegitimate children and finally, the kiss that had almost happened.

Why had he hesitated? Had she imagined the desire in his eyes as they'd danced earlier that night?

Doubts had begun to plague her as soon as Gabriel left. Her experience with men wasn't extensive. Indulging in lighthearted affairs wasn't something she'd ever done. Her friends accused her of being overly conscientious about her reputation, but in fact, she hadn't been attracted to the men in her social circles. She might have worried about her inability to feel physical desire if she hadn't experienced something magical her first year of university.

She'd attended a masquerade party with one of her friends. The event's host was one of London's most notorious bachelors, and it was the last place she should have shown her face. Fortunately, the costumes and masks had enabled her to remain anonymous. The crowd had been racier than she was used to. Drinking and drugs had led to some boisterous behavior and Olivia had made the mistake of getting cornered.

The man had used his size and strength to pin her against the wall and run his hands beneath her skirt. She'd struggled against the hateful press of his moist lips against her throat, but couldn't free herself. And then it had been over and he'd ended up sprawled on the floor some distance away, the hands he cupped over his bloody nose muffling the obscenities he launched at the tall stranger who'd stepped in.

The hallway was too dark for her to see her rescuer clearly and she was still shaken up by the violence of the encounter, but she managed a grateful smile. "Thank you for helping me."

"You don't belong here," the stranger had told her, his English lightly accented. "It isn't safe for someone as young as you are."

Her cheeks had grown hot at his words because he was right and she had felt foolish. "When is it safe for any woman when a man won't stop when she says no?" She peered through the guests, searching for her friend. "Next time I will carry a stun gun instead of lipstick in my purse."

He'd smiled. "Please don't let there be a next time."

"You're right. This isn't my crowd." She had spotted her friend halfway across the room and decided it was time to leave. "It was nice to meet you," she had told him. "I wish the circumstances had been different." Impulsively she rose up on tiptoe and touched her lips to his cheek, before whispering, "My hero."

Before she moved away, he had cupped her cheek and dropped his lips to hers. The touch electrified her and she swayed into his solid strength. His fingers flexed against her skin, pulling her closer. The kiss had been masterful. Demanding enough to be thrilling, but without the roughness that would make her afraid.

Magic, she remembered thinking, as she'd indulged in a moment of reckless daring.

Olivia released a long slow exhale at the memory. Seven

years later it continued to be the most amazing kiss she'd ever had. And she'd never even known his name. Maybe that's why it dwelled so vividly in her memory.

Lying with her forearm across her eyes, Olivia pushed aside the emotions stirred by that singular event. No good would come from dwelling on a romantic moment. The man who rescued her was probably as vile as the rest of the guests and had merely suffered a momentary crisis of conscience. She was marrying an honest, good man and needed to stay focused on the here and now.

As the room began to lighten, Olivia gave up on sleep and pulled out her laptop. During her research into Gabriel and his family, she'd focused on all things Sherdanian. Now she searched for his past romance and discovered a couple articles that mentioned him and Marissa Somme, a half American, half French model he'd dated for several years.

Olivia scanned the news stories. A few mentioned rumors that Gabriel had been considering abdicating the throne to one of his younger brothers, but ultimately, the affair ended instead.

Awash in concern, Olivia went looking for images of the couple. What she saw wasn't reassuring. The news outlets had gotten it right. The couple had been very much in love. Olivia stared at Gabriel's broad grin and Marissa's blinding smile and guessed if she hadn't been a commoner and an unsuitable candidate to give birth to the future king of Sherdana, they would have married and lived happily ever after.

Obviously Gabriel had chosen his country over his heart. And Marissa had vanished.

Hearing soft whispers coming from the bed, Olivia rose from the sofa. Sure enough, the twins were awake. They'd pulled the fluffy cream comforter over their heads, encasing themselves in a cozy cocoon.

For a moment, Olivia envied them each other. An only child, she'd always longed for a sister to share secrets with. If her mother had lived, she could have had a second child and Olivia might not have grown up so isolated from other children. Because her world had been filled with adults—nannies and various tutors—she'd never had a best friend her own age to play with. In fact, playing wasn't something she'd been given much freedom to do.

Multiples obviously ran in the Alessandro family. Did that mean she could expect a set or two of her own to be running around the palace in the years to come?

Olivia tugged on the comforter, pulling it down little by little to reveal the twins. They lay with noses touching, intent on their communication. Their first reaction as the comforter slid away was fear. Olivia saw their hands come together, as they took and received reassurance from each other.

Then, they recognized her and smiled.

"Someone's been sleeping in my bed," she teased, her words bringing forth giggles. "And they're still here."

Then she growled like a big bad bear and reached down to tickle them. Squeals and laughter erupted from the girls, a vast improvement over last night's terrified protests.

Olivia sat down on the bed. The prince would be back soon and the girls needed to be prepared to meet him. No doubt he'd informed the king and queen and they would be interested in meeting their grandchildren. It would be an overwhelming day for the girls and Olivia wanted to prepare them.

"Today you are going to meet many new people," she told them. "I know you might be scared, but you don't need to be."

"A party?"

"Sort of." If that was what it took to keep the twins from being afraid, then so be it.

"A birthday party?"

"No."

"Mommy said."

Bethany's mention of their mother reminded the girls that she was dead. Olivia saw Karina's lip quiver and rushed to distract them.

"Are you this old?" She held up two fingers and was rewarded with head shakes.

"We're this old." Bethany held up one finger.

"But you're too big to be one. I'll bet you have a birthday coming up soon."

"Get pony," Bethany said with a definitive nod.

Olivia rather doubted that, but clever of her to try to sound convincing. "I'm not sure you're old enough for a pony."

Karina spoke for the first time. "Puppy."

That seemed more doable.

"Pony," Bethany repeated. "Mommy said."

"There might be a pony in the stables," Olivia said, aware she was already caving to their demands. She hadn't pictured herself the sort of mother to give in to her child's every whim.

Bethany nodded in satisfaction. "Let's go."

"No." Karina shook her head. "Puppy."

"Oh, no. It's too early to go to the stables. We have to get dressed and have breakfast. Then we have to get you settled in your own room."

"No." Karina's large green eyes brimmed with anxiety.

Immediately Olivia realized what was wrong. "It's okay," she assured them. "The mean lady is gone. You will have really nice people taking care of you."

"Stay here." Bethany had an imperious tone well suited to a princess.

"I'm afraid you can't do that."

"Why not?"

"This is my bed and you two take up way too much room."

"Slept with Mommy."

Somehow they'd circled back to Marissa again. Olivia held her breath as she watched for some sign that they would get sad again, but the girls had discovered the mattress had great springs and they started bouncing and laughing.

Olivia watched them, amusement taking the edge off her exasperation. The challenges confronting her were coming faster than she'd expected. She wasn't just going to become a wife and a princess, but now she was going to take on the role of mother, as well. Not that she couldn't handle all of it. Maybe it was just her sleepless night and her anxiety about marrying a man who might not be over his dead former lover.

While the girls jumped off the bed and raced around the room, looking out the window and exploring the attached bathroom, Olivia heard a soft knock. Assuming it was Libby, she opened the door. To her intense surprise, Gabriel stood there, looking handsome and elegant in a charcoal pinstripe suit, white shirt and burgundy tie.

"I hope it's not too early," he said, entering the room. His gaze slid over her hair and silk-clad body.

Several maids followed, one pushing a cart loaded down with covered plates. Delicious smells wafted in their wake.

Olivia smoothed her hair, acutely aware of her makeup-free face, knowing she wasn't looking her best after such a rough night. She hadn't even brushed her teeth yet.

"No, of course not. You're eager to meet the girls."

"I am." His gaze went past her shoulder, golden eyes intense and a little wary.

Olivia's heart gave a little start as she realized he must be thinking about their mother. Chest tight, she shifted her attention to the twins. "Bethany. Karina. Come meet…" She wasn't sure how to introduce the prince.

Gabriel supplied the description. "Your father."

Beside him, Gabriel felt Olivia tense in surprise. In the hours since leaving her room, he'd contemplated what the best political move would be regarding his daughters and decided he didn't give a damn about the fallout. He intended to claim them.

Olivia held out her hands to the girls and they went toward her. She introduced them one by one, starting with the little girl on her right. "This is Bethany. And this is Karina."

Gabriel could discern no difference between their features. "How can you tell?"

"Bethany is the talkative one."

Neither one was verbal at the moment. They stood side by side wearing matching nightgowns and identical blank stares.

Deciding he would appear less intimidating if he was at their eye level, Gabriel knelt. "Nice to meet you." As much as he longed to snatch them into his arms and hug the breath from their bodies, he kept his hands to himself and gave them his gentlest smile.

The one Olivia had introduced as Bethany eyed him suspiciously for a moment before declaring, "We're hungry." Her imperious tone made her sound like his mother.

"What would you like for breakfast?" he asked them. "We have eggs, pancakes, French toast."

"Ice cream."

"Not for breakfast," he countered.

Olivia made no effort to hide her amusement. Her grin and the laughter brimming in her blue eyes transformed her from an elegant beauty to a vivacious woman. Gabriel felt his eyebrows go up as her charisma lit up the room.

"Wit' chocolate."

Bethany's demands forced Gabriel to refocus his attention. "Maybe after lunch." He'd met some tough negotiators in his time, but none had shown the sort of determination exhibited by his daughters. "If you eat everything on your plate."

"Want ice cream."

"How about waffles with syrup?" He tried softening his words with a smile. The twins weren't moved.

"Olivia." Bethany's plaintive, wheedling tone was charming, and Gabriel found himself struggling to restrain a grin.

"No." Olivia shook her head. "You listen to your father. He knows what's best." She gently propelled the girls toward the table the maid had set for breakfast and got them into chairs. "There aren't any booster chairs so you'll have to kneel. Can you do that?"

The twins nodded and Gabriel pulled out the chair between them, gesturing for Olivia to join them, but she shook her head.

"You should spend some time alone with them. I'm going to shower and get dressed." With one last smile for the twins, she headed toward the bathroom.

As the door shut behind her, Gabriel turned his full attention to the toddlers. "Have you decided what you want to eat?"

Their green eyes steady on him, they watched and waited for some sign that he was weakening. Gabriel crossed his arms over his chest and stared back. He was not going to be outmaneuvered by a pair of toddlers.

"Pancakes."

The word broke the standoff and Gabriel gestured the maid forward to serve pancakes. Having little appetite, he sipped coffee and watched them eat, seeing Marissa in their gestures and sassy attitude.

The girls ate two large pancakes before showing signs of slowing down and Gabriel was marveling at their appetite when the bathroom door opened and Olivia emerged. Her long blond hair framed her oval face in soft waves and she'd played up her blue eyes with mascara and brown eye shadow. She wore a simple wrap dress in seafoam that accentuated her tiny waist and the subtle curves of her breasts and hips. Nude pumps added four inches to her five-foot-six-inch frame and emphasized the sculpted leanness of her calves.

Gabriel felt the kick to his solar plexus and momentarily couldn't breathe. Her beauty blindsided him. Desire raged in his gut. He hadn't expected to feel like this when he proposed. She'd been elegant, poised and cool, inspiring his admiration and appreciation.

In a month she would be legally his. But he was no longer content to wait until his wedding night to claim her. Such had been the heat of his desire for her last night that if the twins hadn't occupied her bed, he would have made love to her.

The strength of his desire gave him a moment's pause. Wasn't this feeling what he'd hoped to avoid when he chose her? Craving something beyond reason was what had gotten him into trouble with Marissa. But desire wasn't love and didn't have to become obsession. He should feel a healthy desire for his future wife. Surely, he could prevent himself from getting in too deep with her and repeating his past mistakes.

He'd sunk into a black depression after his breakup with Marissa. Knowing they couldn't have a future together hadn't prevented him from letting himself be lured into love. He'd come through the other side of losing Marissa, but the fight to come back from that dark place wasn't something he wanted to go through ever again.

"Coffee?" he asked, shoving aside his grim reflections.

He just needed to be certain that he kept a handle on his growing fascination with her. He'd lost his head over Marissa and look what it got him. Two beautiful, but illegitimate, daughters.

"Yes." she gave a little laugh, seeming more relaxed with him than ever before. "I'm afraid I'm in desperate need of the caffeine this morning."

"Rough night?"

"The couch is not as comfortable as it is beautiful."

"Did you get any sleep?"

"Maybe an hour or so." She dished up scrambled eggs, fruit and a croissant. She caught him watching her and gave him a wry smile. "Your pastry chef is sublime. I will need plenty of exercise to avoid becoming fat."

"Perhaps after we speak to my parents about the girls we could take a walk in the garden."

"That would be nice, but I don't think there's time. My schedule is packed with wedding preparations."

"Surely if I can let the country run without my help for half an hour you can delegate some of the wedding preparations to your private secretary. We haven't really had a chance to get acquainted, and with our wedding less than a month away, I thought we should spend some time alone together."

"Is that a command, Your Highness?"

He arched an eyebrow at her playful tone. "Do you need it to be?"

"Your mother is the one who determined my schedule."

Suspecting his fiancée needed no help standing up to the queen, he realized she was chiding him for his neglect during her first week in Sherdana. "I'll handle my mother."

"A walk sounds lovely."

"Go see pony," Bethany declared, shattering the rapport developing between the adults.

"Pony?" Gabriel echoed, looking to Olivia for an explanation.

"Apparently Bethany wants a pony for her birthday. I told her she was too young, but I thought maybe there was a pony in the stables they could visit."

"None that I know of." He saw the bright expectation in their faces vanish and couldn't believe how much he wanted to see them smile again. "But I could be wrong."

He made a mental note to have Stewart see about getting a pair of ponies for the girls. He and all his siblings had all started riding as soon as they could sit up. Ariana was the only one who still rode consistently, but Gabriel enjoyed an occasional gallop to clear his mind after a particularly taxing session of cabinet.

"Do you ride?" he asked Olivia.

"When I visit our country house."

A knock sounded on the door. Olivia's private secretary appeared, Stewart following on her heels. They wore duplicate expressions of concern and Gabriel knew the morning's tranquillity was about to end.

"Excuse me a moment." He crossed the room and pulled Stewart into the hall. "Well?"

"The king and queen are on their way here."

He'd hoped to be the one to break the news to his parents. "How did they find out?"

"The arrival of two little girls in the middle of the night didn't go unnoticed," Stewart told him. "When your mother couldn't find you she summoned me."

"So, you felt the need to spill the whole story."

"The king asked me a direct question," Stewart explained, not the least bit intimidated by Gabriel's low growl. "And he outranks you."

"Gabriel, there you are. I demand to see my granddaughters at once." The queen sailed down the hallway in his direction, her husband at her side. Lines of tension bracketed the king's mouth. After nearly forty years as a queen, nothing disturbed her outward calm. But discovering her son had fathered two illegitimate girls was more stress than even she could graciously handle.

"They've been through a lot in the last few days," Gabriel told her, thinking she would upset the twins in her current state of agitation.

"Have you told Olivia?"

"Last night." He held up a hand when his mother's eyes widened in outrage. "They spent the night with her after she stumbled upon them fleeing their nanny."

The king's light brown eyes had a hard look as they settled on his son. "And how does your future bride feel about it?"

As diplomatic as his parents were with the outside world, when it came to family, they were blunt. It wasn't like them to dance around a question. Of course, they'd never come up against something this enormous before.

"What you want to know is if she intends to marry me despite my having fathered two children I knew nothing about."

"Does she?"

The king's deep frown made Gabriel rein in his frustration. As much as he disliked having his carelessness pointed out, he had let passion overwhelm him to the exclusion of common sense. Marissa had made him wild. She was like no other woman he'd ever met. And because of that their relationship had made his parents unhappy.

Gabriel exhaled harshly. "So far it appears that way."

"Does her father know?" the king asked.

"Not yet. But the girls are living in the house. It won't be long before the truth comes out."

His mother looked grim. "Will Lord Darcy back out on the deal?"

"Olivia doesn't think so. He wants his daughter married to royalty."

"Have you figured out what we're going to say to the press?"

"That they're my daughters," Gabriel said. "We'll send out a press release. Anything else would be a mistake. Olivia noticed the resemblance immediately. They look exactly like Ariana did at that age. Coming clean is a good offensive and hopefully by doing so we can minimize the scandal."

"And if we can't?"

"I'll ride it out."

"We'll ride it out," the king said.

"Have you considered that Olivia might not want to raise Marissa's children?"

Gabriel had already entertained those doubts, but after what he'd seen of Olivia, he'd discovered layers that might surprise everyone. "I don't think that will be an issue. She's already very protective of them and they trust her."

The queen sighed and shook her head. "It *will* be wonderful having children in the palace again. Let's go see your girls."

Four

Olivia was standing with her hands relaxed at her sides as the door opened to admit the king and queen. Libby had warned her they were coming and she'd made sure the girls' hands and faces were clean. The arrival of more unfamiliar people had revived the toddlers' shyness and they hid behind Olivia.

"This is your father's mother," Olivia explained to them, using gentle pressure to nudge them into the open. "She's come to meet you."

Karina shook her head, but Bethany peered at her grandmother. The queen stopped dead at the sight of the girl and reached out a hand to her husband.

"Gabriel, you were right. They look exactly like your sister at that age." She took a seat nearby and gestured Bethany toward her. "What is your name?"

To Olivia's delight Bethany went to the queen.

She stopped just out of arm's reach and studied the queen. "I'm Bethany."

"It's nice to meet you." The queen looked toward her sister. "And what is your name?"

Bethany answered again. "Karina."

"How old are they?" the king asked.

"They'll be two in a few weeks," Gabriel answered.

"Puppy." Karina had finally spoken.

"I have a puppy you can meet. Would you like that?"

The queen smiled as Karina nodded. "Mary," the queen said to the maid who'd brought the twins' clothes from upstairs. "Go get Rosie." The Cavalier King Charles spaniel loved people, especially children, and was a great deal calmer than the queen's vizsla.

In five minutes the maid was back with the dog and both twins were laughing as Rosie licked their cheeks. "Gabriel, why don't you and Olivia make yourself scarce for a while. I'll see the girls are settled."

Recognizing an order when she heard one, Olivia let Gabriel draw her from the bedroom and down the stairs.

"Let's get out of here while we can," he murmured, escorting her through a side door and into the garden.

The late May morning had a slight edge of coolness, but when he offered to send someone upstairs for a sweater, Olivia shook her head.

"Let's walk in the sunshine. I'll warm up fast enough."

He took her hand and tucked it into the crook of his arm. Olivia gave herself up to the pleasure of his strong body brushing against her side as they strolled along the crushed granite pathways.

"Thank you for all you've done with the girls," he said.

"It breaks my heart that they'll grow up without their mother, but I'm glad they have you."

"You never knew yours, did you? She died when you were born?"

She'd never told him that. "I guess we both did our research."

"I've treated our engagement like a business arrangement. For that I'm sorry."

"Don't be. I knew what I was getting into." She heard a touch of cynicism in her tone and countered it with a wry smile.

Gabriel didn't smile back. "I don't think you have any idea what you're getting into."

"That sounds intriguing." Olivia waited for more, but the prince didn't elaborate.

"Starting now I intend to learn everything there is to know about you."

While she was sure he meant to flatter her with the declaration, Olivia froze in momentary panic. What if he found out she hadn't come clean about her past fertility issues? Even with the problem solved, he might be angry that she hadn't disclosed such an important fact.

"A girl needs to keep a little mystery about herself," she countered, gazing up at him from beneath her lashes. "What if you lost interest once you discovered all my secrets?"

"It never occurred to me that you'd have secrets," he murmured, half to himself.

"What woman doesn't?"

"I'd prefer it if we didn't keep secrets from each other."

"After the surprise you received last night, I understand why. So, what would you like to tell me?"

"Me?"

Olivia congratulated herself on turning the conversation back on him. "Getting to know each other was your idea. I thought you'd like to show me how it's done."

Gabriel's eyes gleamed with appreciation. "What would you like to know?"

"Why did you pick me?"

"Your passion for issues relating to children and your tireless determination to make their lives better." Gabriel stopped and turned her to face him. "I knew you would be exactly the sort of queen my country would love."

As his words sank in she stared at the pond, watching the ducks paddle across the still water. "Your country."

At times like this it amused her to think of how many girls longed to be her. If they knew what her life was like, would they still want that? Marriage to a prince might seem like a fairy tale come true, but did they understand the sacrifices to her privacy or the responsibility she would bear?

But marriage into Sherdana's royal family would offer her the opportunity to focus on things near and dear to her heart and to advocate for those who needed help, but who had no one to turn to. Earlier in the week she'd had an opportunity to speak with a local hospital administrator about the need for a more child-friendly space to treat the younger patients. The woman had a lot of ideas how to change the children's ward to make a hospital stay easier on the children as well as their families.

Olivia was excited about the opportunities to help. Sherdana would find her an enthusiastic promoter of solutions for at-risk and underprivileged children. She was proud of the money she'd raised in London and loved the hours she'd spent visiting with children in the hospitals. Their courage in fighting their illnesses always inspired her. She intended to inspire others to help.

As Sherdana's princess and future queen, she would be in the perfect position to bring children's issues to the forefront of public awareness.

"I will do my best to never let your country down."

"I knew you'd say that."

Her knees trembled as he slid his hand beneath her hair, fingertips drawing evocative circles on her nape.

Cupping her cheek in his palm, Gabriel turned her head until their eyes met. Her heart skipped a beat. He wanted her. The expanding warmth in her midsection told her so and she basked in the certainty.

His gaze held her entranced until the second before his lips skimmed hers. Wrenched free of anticipation, relief rushed through her like a wildfire. A groan built in her chest as his tongue traced the seam of her lips. Welcoming the masterful stroke of his tongue into her mouth, she leaned into him, pressing her breasts against his chest, needing his hands to cup their weight and drive her mad.

A throat cleared somewhere behind them. "Excuse me, Your Highness."

Gabriel stiffened and tore his mouth free. Chest heaving, he drew his thumb across her lower lip. "We will continue this later," he promised, his voice a husky rasp against her sensitized nerve endings.

"I look forward to it."

She received the briefest of smiles before he turned to face his private secretary. Released from the compelling grip of his gaze, Olivia had a hard time maintaining her composure. The kiss, although cut short, had been everything a woman craved. Passionate. Masterful. A touch wicked. She locked her knees and moderated her breathing while she listened to Gabriel's conversation with his secretary.

Stewart cleared his throat again. "Sorry to interrupt, but the media found out about your daughters and Lord Darcy is meeting with your parents."

Distantly, she became aware that Stewart was filling in Gabriel rapid-fire style about what had been on the television this morning.

"How did they get wind of it so fast?" Gabriel demanded.

Not even the ice in his voice could banish the lingering warmth Olivia felt from his kiss.

Stewart came up with the most obvious source. "The lawyer might have gone to them."

"Unlikely. He had nothing to gain."

"Someone in the palace, then."

"Who knew last night?"

"The maids who were tasked with preparing the nursery," Stewart said. "But they've worked for the palace for over a decade."

Olivia considered the one who'd been straightening her room at two in the morning. The strangeness of it struck her again, but surely the palace staff was carefully screened and the woman had merely been doing as she said.

"The nanny." Olivia knew with a sinking heart that this had to be the source of the leak. "The one I had escorted off the property."

Stewart considered this. "The lawyer assured me she'd been kept in the dark about the twins' parentage."

"But that was before they'd been brought to the palace," Gabriel said.

"I'm sorry," Olivia murmured, aware she'd committed her first huge mistake as Gabriel's fiancée. "I shouldn't have taken it upon myself to remove her."

"She was the wrong caretaker for the girls and you had their best interests at heart." Gabriel offered her a reassuring nod. "Besides, it was going to be impossible to keep the twins hidden for long."

Although she was accustomed to life in the public eye, she'd never been the focus of such frenzied interest on the part of the media, and the upcoming wedding had stirred them like a cane striking a wasp nest.

"If we present a united front," Olivia said, feeling like his partner for the first time, "I'm sure everything will blow over."

Gabriel took her hand and scorched a kiss across her knuckles. "Then that's exactly what we'll do."

Hand in hand, Olivia and Gabriel entered the salon most often used by the family for its proximity to the back garden and the views of the park beyond. They found Christian and Ariana there. Gabriel caught sight of the television and heard the reporter. The amount of information the news channel had gleaned about the twins' arrival late last night revealed that someone inside the house must have been feeding them information. Gabriel went cold as the reporter speculated on whether or not the powerful Sherdana royal family had paid Marissa to go away or if all along she'd hidden her daughters to keep them from being taken away from her.

"They may be painting us as the bad guys," Christian commented, "but at least they're not claiming we're weak."

Gabriel didn't reply to his brother's remark as Marissa's face came on the screen. As the narrator gave a rundown of her career, Olivia moved as if compelled by some irresistible force, stepping closer to the television. Dismay rose in Gabriel as one after another, the photographs of his former lover on the covers of *Vogue, Elle* and *Harper's Bazaar* flashed on the screen. Her legs looked impossibly long. Her face, incredibly beautiful.

Gabriel knew his daughters would be as exquisite. Would they follow in their mother's footsteps and pursue careers in fashion? Photographers would stand in line to take their picture. They'd make an incredible pair. But was that any way for an Alessandro to make a living?

The question forced Gabriel to consider his daughters' place in his household. They were illegitimate. With their mother's death, that situation could never be rectified. An ache built in his chest for Bethany and Karina. At their age they would retain few memories of their mother. They'd never again know her love.

When the television began showing images of Gabriel and Marissa together, laughing, arms around each other, looking happy and very young, he realized Olivia had gone still. Picture after picture flashed on the screen, and many of them weren't paparazzi shots. There were photos taken of them in private at friends' homes, even a couple when they'd vacationed on a private island in the Caribbean.

Gabriel's disquiet grew as Olivia's attention remained

glued to the news footage that recapped his turbulent years with Marissa. Naturally the reporters made their relationship sound more dramatic, the end more tragic than it actually had been.

While he watched, Olivia's private secretary approached her and spoke softly in her ear. She nodded and came to stand before Gabriel.

"My father wishes to speak to me."

"I'll walk with you."

"You should stay and discuss what is to be done now that the story is out."

Her suggestion made sense, but he wasn't sure it was good to let her leave without clearing the air. "I'd like a moment alone to speak with you."

"I have a fitting for my wedding dress at ten. I should be back a little before noon."

Once again their schedules were keeping them apart. "I have a lunch meeting with my education adviser."

"Perhaps Stewart and Libby can find us a moment to connect later this afternoon."

Gabriel wanted to proclaim they should make time, but had no idea what he was committed to for the rest of the afternoon.

"This shouldn't wait until later. Let's go to my office and discuss this situation in private."

"Whatever you wish."

Disliking the polite calm of her tone, he guided her from the room with a hand at the small of her back. Beneath his palm, her spine maintained a steady inflexibility that marked the change in her mood from their earlier interlude.

As pointless as it was to resent the timing of recent events, Gabriel couldn't stop himself from wishing he and Olivia had been given a month or two to form a personal connection before their relationship had been tested to this extent. But that wasn't the case and as he escorted her into his sanctuary and shut the door, he hoped they could weather this storm without sustaining permanent damage.

His office was on the first floor of the palace, not far from the formal reception room. Originally the space had been one of the numerous salons set aside for visiting guests. Five years ago, he'd appropriated it for his own use, tearing down the lavender wallpaper left over from the late 1970s and installing wood paneling and bookshelves that he'd filled with his favorite authors. The room was his sanctuary.

"You're upset."

"Just concerned about the twins." Her quiet voice and dignified demeanor were at odds with the passionate woman who'd melted in his arms a little while ago. Gabriel felt something tighten in his chest. "I think it might be a good idea to have them in the wedding. I thought I would talk to Noelle Dubone. She's creating my wedding dress and I'm sure she would be happy to design matching flower-girl dresses for Bethany and Karina to wear."

Gabriel leaned back so he could stare into her eyes. "Are you sure?"

"Completely. The world knows they're here. Hiding them would be a mistake."

"I agree. I'll speak with my parents about it." He could tell that Olivia's anxiety over the twins' welfare had been sincere, but surmised more than that was bothering her. "The news coverage about my relationship with Marissa—"

At his slight pause she jumped in. "You looked very happy together." She seemed to have more to say, but remained silent.

"We had our moments." Gabriel drew a deep breath. "But much of the time we fought."

"The paparazzi must not have caught any of those moments on film."

She sounded neutral enough, but Gabriel sensed she

wasn't as tranquil as she appeared. "We fought in private."
And then made up in spectacular fashion.

His thoughts must have shown on his face because her
eyebrows rose.

She moved toward the French doors and looked out.
Gabriel stepped to her side. For a moment he wanted nothing more than to take her in his arms and relive the kisses
from earlier. The compulsion to be near her tested his
composure.

Her gaze slid in his direction. "Passion can be addictive."

How would she know that?

He knew of no serious romances in her life. Her private
life was without even a whiff of scandal. No boyfriends.
No lovers.

"Do you have firsthand knowledge of this fact?" Lord
in heaven, he sounded suspicious. And yet, he couldn't
stop himself from probing. "Have you…?" Realizing what
he'd almost asked, he stopped speaking.

"Taken a lover?"

Damn the woman, she was laughing. Oh, not outwardly
where he could see her mocking smile and take offense.
But inwardly. Her eyes sparkled and her voice had developed a distinct lilt. Had his expression betrayed an unan-
ticipated flare of unfounded jealousy? Or was she reacting
to the revelation that for all his sources, he knew nothing
about her?

Gabriel turned her to face him, but she wouldn't meet
his gaze. "Have you?"

"No." She shook her head. "You'll be my first."

Desire exploded as she met his gaze. Wild with satisfaction that she would be completely his, Gabriel lost touch
with his rational side. Surrendering to the need to kiss her
senseless and show her just how addictive passion could be,

he cupped her cheek in his palm, slid his other hand around her waist to hold her captive and brought his lips to hers.

He gave her just a taste of his passion, but even that was enough to weaken his restraint. Breathing heavily, he set his forehead against hers and searched her gaze.

"Your only." He growled the words.

"Of course."

Her matter-of-fact tone highlighted just how fast he'd let his control slip. His hands fell away, but his palms continued to burn with the heat of her skin. He rubbed them together, determined to banish the lingering sensation.

The need to spend some time alone with her had just grown more urgent. He was concerned that the media storm surrounding the arrival of the twins would make her father consider changing his mind about letting his daughter marry Gabriel. No wedding. No biotech plant on the outskirts of Caron, Sherdana's capital. Gabriel needed to hedge his bets with Olivia.

As long as she still wanted to marry him, everything would proceed as planned. He just needed to reassure her that marrying him was a good idea. And he knew the best way to convince a woman had nothing at all to do with logic.

Some private time should do the trick, just the two of them. A chance to present her with a small token of his affection. Thus far her engagement ring was the only jewelry he'd given her. He should have had a gift ready to present on her arrival in Sherdana, but he'd been preoccupied. And if he was honest with himself, he hadn't been thinking of Olivia as his future bride, but as a next step in Sherdana's economic renaissance.

"I'll arrange for us to have a private dinner in my suite."

"I'll look forward to it," Olivia said, her expression unreadable. Gabriel had chosen her partly because of her composure when dealing with reporters and her public persona. Now, he wasn't happy at not being able to read her.

Shortly after she departed, Gabriel summoned Stewart and had him reschedule his morning appointments so Gabriel could meet with his jeweler. Half an hour later, he entered the reception room where Mr. Sordi waited with two cases of sparkling gems. Despite the wide selection, Gabriel wondered if he'd have trouble selecting the perfect piece for his bride-to-be. In the end, he chose the first bracelet that caught his eye, believing the fanciful design of flowers rendered in diamonds and pink sapphires would please her.

Business concluded, he let Stewart show the jeweler out while Gabriel slipped the bracelet into his office safe. He dashed off a quick note to Olivia, inviting her to dinner, and got one of the maids to deliver it. Then he went off to his lunch meeting with his education adviser, but his thoughts were preoccupied with the evening to come.

After a short conversation with her father to assure him that she'd already known about the twins and was perfectly happy that they'd come to live with their father, Olivia went to change her clothes, but ended up standing on the stone terrace outside her room, staring at the garden below. The euphoria of those passionate moments in Gabriel's arms were misty memories.

Olivia's heart sank to her toes. Caught up in the romance of kissing Gabriel in the beautiful garden, she'd been on the verge of doing things in public she'd never even done in private. While on a subconscious level she'd begun to think in terms of love. In reality she was embarking on an arranged marriage.

Being told Gabriel had loved the mother of his children and being confronted by the hard truth of it were very different animals. The pictures playing across the television screen had complicated her emotions. She'd been besieged by thorny questions.

Had he been thinking of Marissa as he kissed her? Had he been wishing that the woman he'd loved wasn't dead? Or that her ancestry had permitted them to be married? Marissa had been every man's fantasy. Vivacious, sexy, breathtakingly beautiful. In her eyes danced promises she might or might not keep. A man could spend a lifetime wondering which way she would go. How could Olivia hope to compete?

She couldn't.

But she wasn't marrying Gabriel because he loved her. She was marrying him because as a princess her voice advocating for children would reach further and she could fulfill her dream of becoming a mother. Her children would be the next generation of Alessandros. Still, it hurt to see the way Gabriel had stared at the screen as his former lover's face was shown in photo after photo. Her heart had ached at the way his expression turn to stone while his eyes looked positively battered.

Suddenly Olivia wasn't sure she could do this. Sucking in a sharp breath, she glanced down at her engagement ring. Sunlight fell across her hand, lighting up the large center diamond like the fireworks at a centennial celebration. She'd come to Sherdana to marry a prince, not a man, but after tasting passion and realizing she wanted more, she didn't think she could settle for marrying a man with a past that still haunted him.

A man still in love with the mother of his illegitimate twin girls.

Maybe this marriage wasn't meant to be.

But so much was riding on it. So many people were counting on the jobs her father's company would bring to Sherdana. And the wedding was less than a month away. She had a fitting for her dress in less than an hour. Olivia stared at the slim gold watch on her arm, her mother's watch.

A short time later, Olivia stepped out of the car that had driven her and Libby to the small dress shop in Sherdana's historic city center. She'd pushed aside her heavy heart, averse to dwelling on something over which she had no control. She was her father's daughter. Raised as a pragmatist, she knew it was impractical to indulge in pretty dreams of falling in love with her prince and living happily ever after.

The shop door chimed as Olivia entered. Wide windows provided a great deal of light in the small but elegant reception room. The walls had been painted pale champagne to complement the marble floors. There was a gold damask-covered sofa flanked by matching chairs in the front room. The glass-topped coffee table held a portfolio of Noelle Dubone's previous work. Some of her more famous clients were not featured in the book, but on the walls. Stars, models, heiresses, all wearing Noelle's gorgeous gowns.

Almost before the door shut behind them, Noelle was on hand to greet her. The designer offered Olivia a warm smile and a firm handshake.

"Lady Darcy, how delightful to see you again."

Noelle had a lilting Italian accent. Although Sherdana shared borders with both France and Italy, it had chosen Italian as its official national language. With her dark hair and walnut-colored eyes, Noelle's lineage could have gone back to either country, but from earlier conversations Olivia knew the designer's ancestry could be traced back to the 1500s. Noelle might not be one of Sherdana's nobility, but the church kept excellent records.

"It's good to see you, as well," Olivia said, warming to the willowy designer all over again. Choosing to have a dress made by Noelle had been easy in so many ways. Although her London friends had counseled Olivia to go with a more famous designer and have an extravagant gown made, Olivia had decided she much preferred Noelle's artistry. Plus Noelle was Sherdanian. It made political sense for Olivia to show her support of the country where she would soon be a princess, especially taking into consideration how hard-hit Sherdana's economy had been in the past few years.

"I have your dress waiting in here." Noelle showed Olivia into a dressing room.

For her more famous clients, Noelle often traveled for fittings. She would have brought the dress to the palace if Olivia had requested. But Olivia liked the shop's cozy feel and wasn't eager to entertain anyone's opinion but her own.

The dress awaiting her was as beautiful as she remembered from the sketches. It had stood out among the half dozen Noelle had shown her six months ago; in fact, the rendering had taken her breath away.

With the help of Noelle's assistants, Olivia donned the dress. Facing the three-way mirror, she stared at her reflection, and was overcome with emotion. It was perfect.

From the bodice to her thighs, the dress hugged the lean curves of her body. Just above her knees it flared into a full skirt with a short train. Made of silk organza, embroidered with feathery scrolls over white silk, the gown's beauty lay in its play of simple lines and rich fabrics. Although Noelle had designed the dress to be strapless, Olivia had requested some sort of small sleeve and the designer had created the illusion of cap sleeves by placing two one-inch straps on either shoulder.

"What are planning to do for a veil?" Noelle asked.

"The queen is lending me the tiara she wore on her wedding day," Olivia said. "I'm not sure I want to use a veil with it."

"Good. When I designed the dress, I didn't picture it with a veil." Noelle stepped back to admire her handiwork.

"You have lost a little weight since we measured you. The waist needs to be taken in a little."

Olivia turned sideways to peer at the way the short train looked behind her. "I will try not to gain before the wedding."

For the next hour, Noelle and her staff worked on minor alterations to the fit. While Olivia thought the dress fit well enough that she could have worn it as is, Noelle was obviously a perfectionist.

"I have another project that I'd like to talk to you about," Olivia said as Noelle handed off the dress to her assistant.

Ever since arriving, she'd been thinking about including the twins in the wedding. While Gabriel seemed okay with the idea, she wasn't sure how his family would react, but after this morning's media coverage of the girls' arrival at the palace, hiding them from public scrutiny would be impossible and counterproductive.

"Come into my office," Noelle said. "Tell me what you have in mind."

Sipping the coffee Noelle's assistant had provided, Olivia contemplated the best way to begin, then decided to just dive in.

"Did you happen to see the news this morning?"

"About Prince Gabriel's daughters?" Noelle pressed her lips together. "The royal family hasn't given them much fodder for stories in the last few years. I'm afraid the level of coverage on this particular item so close to your wedding is just too huge for them to use restraint."

"Dealing with the media comes with the territory," Olivia said. "You'd know that."

Noelle looked startled for a second. "I only design for the stars," she demurred. "I'm not one of them myself."

"You are making a name for yourself. Don't be surprised when you become as big a story as your clients."

"I hope that doesn't happen. I like my quiet little life."

Noelle's gaze touched a silver frame on her desk. It held the photo of a small dark-haired boy. The angle didn't offer a very good view of his face, but Olivia could tell from Noelle's expression that he was very special to her.

"Is he your son?"

"Yes. Marc. He was two in that picture. The same age as the prince's daughters."

Olivia felt a clenching low in her abdomen. A cry from her empty womb. "He's beautiful. How old is he now?"

"Almost four."

Olivia didn't ask about the boy's father. She knew Noelle wasn't currently married and wasn't sure if the question would arouse difficult memories.

"I would like to include Prince Gabriel's daughters in the wedding and want you to make dresses for them."

"I'll work on some sketches and send them over to the palace. Did you have a color in mind?"

"White with pale yellow sashes. To match Princess Ariana's gown." The color suited the dark-haired princess and would her nieces, as well.

"I'll get to work immediately."

At the sound of a light knock, both women looked toward the door. Noelle's assistant hovered on the threshold.

"I just wanted to let you know that there are media outside."

Although the announcement of her engagement to Gabriel had briefly made Olivia newsworthy in England, the future princess of a small country hadn't interested the British press for long.

In Sherdana, however, it was a different story. She'd found the citizens were very curious about her. When she'd visited three months ago, she'd been besieged by requests for interviews and followed wherever she went. Numerous public appearances had filled her daily schedule from ribbon-cutting ceremonies to attending sessions of parliament.

But when Olivia emerged into Noelle's reception room, she understood the assistant's concern. At least a hundred people crowded the streets, most of them armed with cameras. Surely not all these people were reporters. David, her driver, and Antonio, the enormous man Gabriel had assigned to accompany her whenever she was out in public, had called in five others from palace security to create a corridor of safety between the front door of the wedding shop and the car.

Olivia shot Libby a look. "I think life as I knew it has come to an end." Then she turned to Noelle. "Thank you for everything. The dress is perfect."

"You're welcome."

Squaring her shoulders, Olivia put on her public face and stepped toward the front door. Noelle held it open for her with a whispered, *"Bon courage."*

"Olivia, how are you dealing with the discovery of the prince's illegitimate children?"

"Lady Darcy, can you tell us if the wedding is still on?"

"How do you feel about raising another woman's children?"

"Do you think the prince would have married Marissa if he'd been able?"

The questions rained down on Olivia as she headed for the car, smiling and waving as she walked, but responding to none. She slipped each query into its own special cubbyhole for later retrieval and didn't realize she was holding her breath until the car had pulled away from the curb. Libby watched her in concern.

"I'm fine."

"You look…unhappy."

"I'm just tired. The twins slept in my bed and I wasn't able to get comfortable on the couch. That's all."

The excuse pacified her secretary and gave Olivia the space to sort through the highs and lows of the last twenty-four hours. While she wasn't naive enough to think that Gabriel was marrying her for anything other than business, Olivia had hoped that he'd grow fond of her. But while they'd kissed in the garden, she'd let herself believe that their future could be filled with passion and romance.

The photos of him with Marissa that the media had broadcast this morning had been a wake-up call. That was love. Olivia stared out the window at the old town slipping past.

She needed time to adjust to sharing him with a ghost.

Five

When Olivia returned to her room after the fitting, she discovered an invitation and a small, slender box wrapped in ribbon. Heart pounding, she opened the envelope and recognized Gabriel's strong handwriting.

A quiet dinner, just the two of them. In his suite. She clutched the stationery to her chest and breathed deep to calm her sudden attack of nerves. Except for the brief time last night and this morning, they hadn't been alone together. Did he intend to seduce her? Olivia certainly hoped so, but what did she wear to her deflowering? Something demure that matched her level of experience in all things sexual? Something that bared her skin and invited his touch?

Her fears that he didn't find her attractive had melted beneath the heat of this morning's kiss. But he was accustomed to women with far more experience than she possessed. Apprehension made her nerves buzz like a swarm of angry hornets.

Leaving her worries to sort themselves out, she tugged at the ribbon holding the box closed. The pale blue silk fell away. Her fingers brushed the hinged lid as she savored the anticipation of her first gift from Gabriel. From the box's shape, she knew it was a bracelet.

Olivia took a deep breath and opened the lid. Lying on a bed of black velvet was a stunning free-form emerald an inch and a half wide and almost two inches long that dominated the design. The rest of the band was diamonds, set in a diamond-shaped pattern. Bold and contemporary, it wasn't the sort of thing she'd wear, being a little too trendy, but she couldn't fault Gabriel's taste.

Ignoring a pang of disappointment that he'd chosen something so not her taste, she draped the wide cuff over her wrist. As she admired the sparkle, she couldn't shake a nagging sense of familiarity. It was a unique piece, something one-of-a-kind, yet she was certain she'd seen it before. But where? The answer eluded her and she set aside her musings as Libby arrived and helped Olivia decide on the perfect outfit to highlight Gabriel's extravagant gift.

Around midafternoon she went up to the nursery and found the twins eager to visit the stables. But she listened with only half her attention as Bethany chattered on the short walk to the stables. Olivia was having a hard time thinking about anything except her dinner with Gabriel and the hope that they could forget all about Marissa and begin their lives together. Comparing herself to Gabriel's former lover would only lead to trouble down the road. She'd be smarter to put that energy into keeping Gabriel's mind fixed on the present.

While a pair of grooms took Bethany and Karina to look at the ponies their father had ordered to be delivered to the stable, Olivia drifted along the barn's center aisle, stroking a soft nose here and there, lost in a pleasant daydream. The soothing sounds of the barn wrapped her in a cocoon of stillness that allowed her ample privacy to relive the moments in the garden that morning.

Her blood heated and slowed, flowing into the sensitive area between her thighs that Gabriel's fervent kiss had awakened earlier. She leaned her back against a stall and closed her eyes to better relive the delicious caress of his hands against her back and hips. Her breasts had ached for his possession. She'd never felt anything like the powerful craving his kiss aroused. She'd been seconds away from begging him to touch her everywhere. He'd been her master. Her teacher. And she, a very willing student.

The memories disturbed the smooth rhythm of her breathing. How was it possible that just thinking of Gabriel aroused her?

"Are you okay?"

Olivia's eyes snapped open. A groom peered at her, concern in his brown eyes.

She offered a weak smile, feeling heat in her cheeks, put there by her sensual daydreams. Had she really been standing in the middle of a barn, imagining how it would feel to have Gabriel's large, strong hands roaming over her bare skin?

"Fine." The word came out a little garbled. What magic had he wrought to make her forget her surroundings so completely? "I'm fine."

From outside came the twins' high-pitched voices lifted in childish delight. Olivia pushed away from the wall and went in search of them. In the stable yard, beneath the watchful eyes of the grooms who'd taken charge of them, they each stood on a mounting block in order to better acquaint themselves with their new pony.

Olivia fought anxiety as she watched the girls, but soon she calmed down. These ponies had obviously been chosen for their placid demeanor; otherwise the excited movements of the twins would have startled them. The geldings were well matched in size, color and markings. Bethany's had a long, narrow blaze that stretched from forehead to right between his nostrils. Karina's had a wider stripe of white that spread out as it reached the nose. Both ponies had two white front socks and one back.

Bethany was the first to notice Olivia. She threw her

arms around the pony's neck and said in an excited voice. "Look at my horse. Her name is Grady."

Olivia started to correct Bethany on the gender of her new pony, but Karina jumped in before she could speak.

"Peanut." The quieter twin looked so delighted that Olivia wondered if she would still demand a puppy for her birthday.

"They're lovely," Olivia said. "But I think they're both boys."

The girls were too excited to listen and went back to petting and chattering to their ponies. The head groom came over to where Olivia stood.

"They will make fine horsewomen."

"I believe you're right."

"Would you like to see the mount His Highness chose for you?"

It had never occurred to Olivia that she would receive a horse as well when she told Gabriel how she loved to ride whenever she spent time at Dansbrooke. The park around the palace wasn't as extensive as the lands surrounding her family's country estate, but she welcomed the opportunity to get whatever exercise she could.

"I'd love to see him." She laughed. "Or her."

"It's a mare. A Dutch Warmblood. I heard you've done some eventing. You'll find Arioso is a wonderful jumper and an eager athlete."

The beautiful chestnut had large, soft eyes and a gentle disposition, but before she had time to do more than stroke the mare's long neck, the twins had finished with their ponies and joined her at the stall.

Deciding they'd had enough for one day, Olivia gathered them together and bid the grooms goodbye. After depositing them with a pair of maids in the nursery, she returned to her room to bathe and dress.

Olivia took a long time preparing for the evening. She

played with hairstyles for an hour before settling on a softly disheveled updo that required only a couple of pins to keep it in place. The gown she'd chosen was a simple black sheath that bared her arms and appeared demure in the front but dipped low in the back.

Anticipation began to dissolve her calm as she zipped up the dress and fastened simple diamond dangles to her earlobes. Boldly eschewing panty hose, she slid her feet into elegant patent leather pumps.

She wanted everything about her to say "touch me."

And surveying her appearance in the full-length mirror, Olivia felt confident she'd done just that. That left only one more thing to do. Olivia popped the top on the jewelry box and laid the wide bracelet across her wrist. Libby helped by securing the clasp.

"Is this all for my brother's benefit?" Ariana had slipped into the room after a soft knock.

Olivia felt her cheeks heating. "Do you think he'll approve?"

Ariana smiled. "How could he not?" Her gaze slipped over Olivia, stopping at the diamond-and-emerald bracelet. She reached for Olivia's hand, as the color drained from her face. "Where did you get that?"

"Gabriel sent it to me." Concern rose in Olivia. Why was Ariana looking as if she'd seen a ghost? "Why? Do you recognize it?"

"Gabriel sent it?" Ariana echoed. She shook her head. "I don't understand."

"You recognize it?" Olivia felt her heart hit her toes. "It's cursed, isn't it?"

"You might say that."

"Tell me."

"It's none of my business."

There was no way she was letting Ariana get away

without an explanation. "If there's something wrong, I need to know."

"Really, I shouldn't have said anything." Ariana backed toward the bedroom door. "I'm sure everything is fine."

It wasn't like Ariana to hedge, especially when it came to things that distressed her. And seeing the bracelet had obviously upset the princess.

"What do you mean everything is fine? Why wouldn't it be? What aren't you telling me about the bracelet?"

Olivia caught Ariana's wrist in a tight grip. Startled, the brunette looked from the hand holding her, to the bracelet on Olivia's wrist and finally met her gaze.

"I don't want to upset you."

"And you think that's going to persuade me to let you walk out of here without spilling the truth?" Olivia tugged her future sister-in-law toward the wingback chairs flanking the fireplace. She didn't let go until Ariana sat down. "Tell me what about the bracelet upset you."

Releasing an audible sigh, the princess leveled her pale gold eyes on Olivia. "The last time I saw that bracelet was the night before Gabriel broke things off with Marissa."

Pain lanced through Olivia, sharper than anything she'd experienced this morning as she'd watched the pictures of Gabriel and Marissa on the television.

"He bought it for her."

"Yes. It was…for their second anniversary."

The cool platinum burned like acid against Olivia's skin. She clawed at the clasp, blood pounding in her ears. Her excitement over having dinner alone with Gabriel vanished, replaced by wrenching despair. The first gift he'd given her had been the bracelet he'd bought to celebrate two years with Marissa?

The clasp popped open beneath her nails. Olivia dropped it on the mantle and sat in the chair opposite

Ariana, unsure how much longer her shaky legs would support her.

"How did he get it back?"

"I don't know. Maybe she returned it when they broke up."

Olivia felt sick. It was bad enough that Gabriel had given her the trinket he'd bought for another woman, it was worse that it was a returned gift. "I thought I'd seen it before," she murmured.

Ariana leaned forward and placed her hand over Olivia's. "I'm sure this is all a huge misunderstanding. Maybe I'm thinking of a different bracelet."

Olivia drew comfort from Ariana for a moment, before sitting up straight and bracing her shoulders. "The only misunderstanding is mine. I thought tonight was supposed to be the beginning of something between us." She offered Ariana a bitter smile. "I forgot that our marriage is first and foremost a business arrangement."

"I don't believe that's true. I saw the way Gabriel watched you this morning. He was worried by how you reacted to the press coverage of the twins' arrival and all the scandal it stirred up."

"He's worried about losing the deal with my father."

"Yes, but there's more to it than that. He had other opportunities to secure Sherdana's economic future. He chose you."

Ariana's words rang with conviction, but Olivia shook her head. The sight of the bracelet made her long to hurl it into the deepest ocean. She felt betrayed and yet she had no right. She was marrying Gabriel because he was handsome and honorable and she would one day become a queen. Her reasons for choosing him were no more romantic than his.

"Ask him to tell you about the first time you met."

"The party at the French embassy?" Olivia recalled

his stiff formality and their brief, stilted conversation, so different from their exchange in the garden this morning.

"Before that."

Olivia shook her head. "We didn't meet before that."

"You did. You just don't remember."

How was that possible? Every time he drew near, her stomach pitched and her body yearned for his touch. His lips on hers turned her into an irrational creature of turbulent desires and rollicking emotions. If they'd met, she'd have recognized the signs.

"Your brother is very memorable," she argued. "I'm certain you are mistaken."

Ariana's eyes glowed. "Just ask him."

Abruptly filled with uncertainty, Olivia looked down at her gown and noticed the brush of cool air against her bare back and arms. She'd dressed to entice Gabriel. She'd wanted his hands to go places no man had ventured before. Even after learning that he'd given her a bracelet that once belonged to his former lover, she still wanted him. She ached with yearning. Burned with hungers unleashed by an hour in the bath tracing her naked skin with her fingertips, imagining Gabriel doing the same.

"Damn it." The curse shot out of her and startled Ariana.

"Oh, I've really done it," the princess muttered. "Please don't be mad at Gabriel. That was five years ago. I'll bet he doesn't even remember the bracelet."

Olivia's gaze sharpened into focus as she took in Ariana's miserable expression. "You remembered."

"I'm a woman. I have an artist's eye for detail." Ariana shook her head. "Gabriel is a man. They don't notice things like fashion. Now, if he'd given you a set of antlers off a buck he'd shot, that he'd recall."

Olivia recognized that Ariana was trying to lighten her mood, but the damage had been done. She wasn't half as angry with Gabriel as she was with herself. For being a fool. For not realizing that she never would have agreed to marry Gabriel unless she was already emotionally engaged.

But it was too late. She was already in too deep. The only thing she could do now was keep her wits about her and not allow herself to be disappointed again.

To his intense shock, Gabriel was second-guessing himself.

As he towel-dried his hair. As he shaved for the second time that day. As he dressed in gray slacks and a black collarless button-down shirt.

All he could think about was what a mistake he'd made with the bracelet he'd chosen for Olivia's first present. As beautiful as the item was, he couldn't help but think she'd appreciate something more romantic with a little history attached.

He was grimly amused with himself. Since when had he devoted this much time and energy to a gift for a woman? In Marissa's case, he'd always zeroed in on the most flamboyant piece available, the more expensive the better, and been richly rewarded for his generosity.

Gabriel slid a watch onto his wrist and checked the time. He had half an hour before Olivia was due to arrive if he wanted to fetch a particular piece from the vault. "I have a quick errand to run," he told Stewart. "If Lady Darcy arrives before I return, serve her a glass of champagne and assure her I won't be long."

With that, he exited his suite and headed to the vault, his mind on the perfect thing to present to his fiancée. It took him exactly ten minutes to find the necklace and return. Stewart was alone when Gabriel returned.

"Dinner is set to be served at eight."

"Perfect." Gabriel had no interest in rushing. At the

same time, he wanted plenty of the evening left over for getting to know Olivia thoroughly. "You ordered all her favorites?"

"Of course." Stewart's head turned at the light knock on the door. "That must be Lady Darcy. I'll let her in, then make myself scarce."

Gabriel grinned, glad she was as eager to begin their evening as he. Stewart went to answer the door. With his pulse kicked into overdrive, Gabriel found himself holding his breath in anticipation. Realizing what he was doing, he exhaled, wondering how long it had been since the idea of spending time alone with a woman had excited him. But Olivia wasn't just any woman.

She aroused him faster and more intensely than anyone since Marissa. To look at her, it made no sense. She was elegant, cool and poised. Not the sort of sultry, lush temptress that turned men's heads. But today he'd discovered an inner core of vibrant, sensual woman hiding within her. The little he'd sampled explained his craving for a more prolonged taste.

A tense conversation was taking place near the door. Gabriel frowned as he spied the petite woman standing in the hall. Not Olivia. Her private secretary. Although curious about the content of their discussion, Gabriel made no attempt to listen in. He would learn what it was about soon enough.

The exchange at the door came to an end. Stewart came toward him, wearing a frown.

"What's wrong?"

"Your Highness." Stewart looked as if an elephant had stepped on his toes. "Lady Darcy has declined your invitation."

Dumbstruck, Gabriel stared at his assistant. Declined his invitation? Outrageous.

He'd anticipated their evening alone and the chance to learn more about her. "Is she ill?"

Stewart hesitated. "I didn't…get that impression."

"What impression did you get?" he demanded, impatient at his secretary's caginess.

Stewart squared his shoulders. "That perhaps she was unhappy…with you."

"With me?" When they'd parted this morning she'd been all dreamy eyes and feminine wiles. What could have possibly happened in the past twelve hours?

Without another word to Stewart, Gabriel exited his suite. Long, determined strides carried him down the hall toward the rooms assigned to Olivia. He barely noticed the maid scurrying out of his way as he passed her. He did, however, notice Ariana stepping out of Olivia's suite.

"Gabriel, what are you doing here?"

"I'm here to collect Olivia for dinner."

Ariana's gold eyes widened. "Didn't you get the message? Olivia's not up to having dinner with you tonight."

He leaned down and pinned his sister with a steely glare, wondering what mischief she had been up to. "What's wrong with her?"

Ariana set her hand on her hip and regarded him with annoyance. "She's not feeling well."

"Then I'd be remiss in not checking on her," Gabriel intoned, sounding as suave as he could through gritted teeth. "Step aside."

But his sister didn't budge. "Leave it tonight, Gabriel," she coaxed. "Give her a little time."

"Time for what?"

"Honestly," his sister fumed. "You can be so insensitive sometimes."

What was he missing? "Enlighten me."

Ariana pressed her lips together, but Gabriel kept up his

unrelenting stare and she finally sighed. "She's had your affair with Marissa thrown in her face all day."

He remembered the expression on Olivia's face while the footage of him and Marissa had played on the television. But he thought they'd cleared the matter up in his office. Why was she letting the past bother her? Gabriel nudged his sister aside and reached for the door handle.

"Gabriel—"

"This is none of your concern. It's between me and my future bride."

"Fine." Ariana tossed up her hands. "But don't say I didn't warn you."

With her dire words ringing in his ears, Gabriel entered Olivia's suite. Some impulse prompted him to slip the lock before scanning the space. His fiancée was not in the bedroom. After his encounter with Ariana, he'd expected to find Olivia sulking over some perceived slight. Then he noticed a slight billowing of the sheer curtains over the French doors leading out onto the terrace.

Olivia stood near the terrace railing staring out over the pond and the park, her gaze on the path where they'd walked and kissed this morning. She wore a black dress that bared her back in a plunging V. She'd knotted her hair on top of her head, exposing the nape of her neck. The sight of all that bare skin did unruly things to his body. He'd always been a sucker for a woman's back, finding the combination of delicacy and strength an intoxicating combination.

Gabriel shoved aside desire and refocused on the reason he'd come here in the first place.

"We're supposed to be having dinner in my suite."

"I don't feel up to it," she replied in a cool tone, not bothering to turn around.

"Then you're not upset."

"Of course not."

He didn't believe her. For the briefest of moments he wondered if she was trying to manipulate him with some feminine trickery. He almost laughed at the notion. Marissa was the only other woman who'd tried to best him with her wiles. He'd quickly set her straight.

Time to set Olivia straight, as well. "I thought this morning you understood that whatever was between Marissa and me has been over for three years."

"What sort of evening did you have in mind for us tonight?" She turned around and faced him and he got his first glimpse of her expression. Genuine anger shimmered in her gaze. "Were we to sip champagne and become lovers or did you plan to educate me on Sherdana's upcoming social and economic challenges?"

What had gotten into her? This morning she'd been like warm honey in his arms. Tonight she'd become an ice sculpture. All this because a few reporters dredged up old news from three years ago?

"I'd hoped we'd spend some time getting to know each other tonight, but I had no intention of rushing you into bed." Tired of sparring with her, he stepped within touching distance. "I thought that we'd reached an understanding this morning."

"So did I," she murmured, the fire fading from her tone.

"Then what's wrong?"

"Our marriage is an arrangement."

"Yes." He grazed his fingertips up her sides from her hips, letting them coast along the side of her breasts. The hitch in her breath told him the fight was over. "But it doesn't have to be all business between us."

"And it isn't," she agreed. "It's just that I'm not really sure what's happening."

So, he wasn't the only one struggling to find his way. Ever since last night, he'd found himself drawn to her as never before, but he wasn't sure she felt it, too. And now that he knew she did, he wasn't about to let her run away from it.

"We have strong sexual chemistry," he told her, and then in a softer voice confessed, "I wasn't expecting that."

Her scent flowed around him, feminine and enticing. As desire began to assert itself, he noticed the details his anger had blinded him to. For a woman intent on denying him her company, she'd dressed with care. He dipped his head and drank in the feminine scent of her. She'd dabbed a light floral perfume behind her ears. His lips found the spot and made her shiver.

"Gabriel, please." Her hand on his chest wasn't going to deter him now that he'd gotten wind of her imminent surrender.

"Please, what?" he inquired. "Stop?"

Knowing it was what she had in mind, he tugged the pins from her hair and tossed them aside. The golden waves spilled around her face and shoulders.

"Yes." But the word lacked conviction.

"You're lying," he pressed. "And badly. This is what you wanted when you dressed tonight." He took her stiff body in his arms and immediately the fight began to drain from her muscles. "My hands on you." He dipped his head and drew his lips across her cheek, finishing his thought with his breath puffing against her ear. "My mouth tasting your skin."

Her body was limp against him now, all resistance abandoned.

"We're meant to be together." He was more convinced of that than ever. "You know it as well as I do."

She'd closed her eyes to hide from him, not realizing how futile her actions were. "Yes."

Six

Without sight, all her other senses came to life. The unsteady rasp of Gabriel's breath told her he too was disturbed by the attraction between them. But was it enough? Hadn't she discovered less than an hour ago that she wanted more from him? So much more.

His fingertips grazed along the sensitive skin inside her arm, from the hollow behind her elbow to the pulse jerking frantically in her wrist. Gently he laced their fingers and began to pull her along the terrace. Her eyes flew open.

"Where?" Her gaze found his and she saw feverish hunger blazing in the bronze depths.

"To bed, of course," he teased, but there was nothing lighthearted about the determined set of his mouth or the tension that rode his muscles. Tension that communicated across the short distance between them.

"What about dinner?"

Inside the suite once more, he drew her close, sliding a hand over her hip to pull her against the hard jut of his erection, and bent to whisper in her ear. "You made me hungry for something besides food."

His lips dropped to hers, lingering at the corner of her mouth for too long. His unproductive nuzzling wasn't getting the job done. She wanted a kiss. A real, hard, deep kiss with no possibility of interruption. Growling low in her throat, she lifted on tiptoe and framed his face with her hands, holding him still while she pressed her mouth to his. Her tongue tested the seam of his lips as she flattened her breasts against Gabriel's broad chest, eager to convey her desire, letting her hunger shine through.

Gabriel captured handfuls of the dress near her shoulder blades and pulled the edges forward and down, baring her torso to the waist. Olivia gasped at the sudden rush of cool air over her breasts.

He slid his hands up over her rib cage until his fingers reached the undersides of her breasts. Smiling with male satisfaction, he cupped her and kneaded slightly.

She arched into the pressure of his hands, offering herself to him. Reaching behind, she found the dress's zipper and slid it down. With a determined stroke of her palms against her hips, the dress pooled at her feet, leaving her wearing nothing but her black pumps and a white lace thong.

He had tracked the progression of the dress to the floor, his gaze sliding over her legs as the falling black fabric bared her to him. Liking the way his nostrils flared at the sight of her nakedness, Olivia stepped out of the dress and kicked it aside.

Pressure built inside her as she hooked her fingers in the thong, determined to rid herself of it, as well. Gabriel's hands covered hers, halting her actions.

"This is your first time." His voice sank into rich, warm tones that did little to equalize her pulse or diminish her hunger. "I want to take this slow."

"I don't."

His lips moved into a predator's smile, slow and lazy. "You'll thank me later."

And with that, he swept her feet off the floor.

Placing her in the center of the big bed, Gabriel stepped back to rid himself of his clothes. Olivia raised herself on her elbows to better catch the unveiling of all that amazing bronze skin. From the little contact she'd had with his body, she knew he was lean and well-muscled, but nothing prepared her for the chiseled perfection of his torso as his shirt buttons gave way. She goggled at the sheer beauty of his broad shoulders and the sculptured magnificence of his chest.

He raised his eyebrows at her obvious curiosity, his hands going to the belt buckle. As he unfastened the top button, he kicked off his shoes. His pants hit the floor, followed by his socks.

He left on his boxers, but Olivia's eyes were drawn to the way they bulged in front. Her obvious curiosity and lack of concern turned him on and sped even more blood to his groin. Making this the most amazing night of her life might prove challenging. She certainly wasn't playing the part of nervous virgin.

He climbed onto the bed.

"What's this?" His finger grazed a black Chinese character in the hollow beside her hip bone and her stomach muscles twitched.

"A tattoo."

His elegant British fiancée had a tattoo? And in a very sexy spot, he might add. He frowned.

"What does it say?"

"Hope." She bent the leg opposite him and braced her foot on the mattress so she could cant her hips toward him. "I got it in college. My one wild act freshman year."

He imagined her baring her body for the needle, sliding down jeans and underwear. And the thought of another man touching her there made him want to roar in outrage.

His emotions must have shown on his face because she rushed to say, "It was done by a woman."

His shoulders relaxed at her words. She was his, or would be soon. And he wasn't the sort of man who cared to share. Living with two brothers had turned him into a possessive madman when anything encroached on what he believed was his.

"In that case, it's very sexy."

She grinned at how grudging his words sounded. It continued to both infuriate and delight him that she was not even remotely close to the type of woman he thought he'd chosen to make the next queen of Sherdana and his wife.

He hadn't anticipated surprises. He'd expected gracefulness and composure, not this wanton creature with her disheveled hair, bare breasts and body marked by the word *hope*. But now that he had her, she turned him inside out with wanting. She fired his imagination and his blood in the span of a heartbeat. Life would not be dull with her.

Which was the problem. He'd had passion once, crazy desire. It had consumed him and compelled him to think with every part of him but the one that mattered for the future king of Sherdana: his head. He didn't need a wife who made him feel out of control. He needed someone sensible, who kept him focused on matters of state.

Yet deep down he knew Olivia would do that.

And then, behind the closed doors of their private suite, she would make him forget everything but the sweet rush of carnal pleasure.

The best of both worlds.

What was there to worry about?

Taking her leg in his hand, he caressed upward from her knee to the place where her thighs came together.

"That's…" Her voice faltered as he slid one finger beneath the scrap of lace hiding her hot, wet center from him. She balled her fists into the coverlet, holding her breath as the tip of his finger grazed her warmth.

"You are incredibly wet," he said, delighted by the quickness of her arousal.

"Stop talking and touch me."

"Like this?" Stripping off her underwear, he did as she

asked, dipping between the folds that concealed her core and riding the river of wetness toward the knot of nerves. He circled it slowly, listening to her pant, smelling the waves of her arousal. Her hips rose off the mattress, pushing into his hand.

Gorgeous.

With her eyes closed, her knuckles whitening as she held on to the bed linens for dear life, she was as deep into the throes of sensual pleasure as any woman he'd ever known. She writhed against his hand, mindless in her pursuit of her ultimate goal. He watched her face, absorbing each tremble and jerk of her body as he carried her closer and closer to orgasm. Her brow knit as she concentrated. He picked up the pace and watched her mouth open, her back arch.

It was the sexiest thing he'd ever seen.

And it was his name that escaped her lips as she climaxed.

Panting, she opened her eyes. "That was incredible."

He grinned. "It gets better."

"Better?" She sounded doubtful. "I can't imagine that it could get better than that."

He loved a challenge. "Hold your opinion for another hour or so."

"An hour?" She stared at him, her eyes wide with uncertainty. "I don't think I could possibly survive that long."

He didn't think he would survive that long, either. But he was determined to try.

Forking his fingers into her hair, he brought his mouth to hers. Desire continued to claw at him, and tasting her eagerness only made it that much harder for him to maintain control.

He wanted to claim her, make her his. The notion that he was the first man to put his hands on her made him wild. The uncivilized part of him that had run wild with

Marissa roared within its cage, demanding to be free. Gabriel turned his back on those impulses.

Making this first time perfect for her was the only thing that mattered. And for him to do that, he must stay in control.

Her hands left the mattress and moved up his sides. Caresses like fire swept over his skin as she explored the contours of his shoulders and back.

His tongue delved between her parted lips, tasting her passion, capturing the soft cries she made as his fingers found her breasts, nails raking lightly over her taut nipples. Her legs tangled with his. Her wet curls dampened his boxers. He rocked against her heat and broke off the kiss to take her nipple in his mouth.

Her head fell back as he suckled her. Cupping her butt in his hand, he guided her undulating rhythm until they were in sync. A groan collected in his chest as her fingers speared beneath the waistband of his boxers and found him.

Olivia gasped at the first contact with Gabriel's erection. The silken feel of his skin. The steel beneath. The sheer size of him made her whimper with fear and excitement. How was she supposed to take all of him inside her?

"It's okay," he murmured, easing her fingers away. Somehow he'd understood what was in her mind. "I'll take it slow. You'll get the chance to get used to me little by little."

"But you aren't little, so little by little isn't how I see this happening," she retorted, twisting one hand free so she could touch him again.

A groan burst from him as she wrapped her hand fully around his length and measured him from tip to base.

He pulled her hand away and pinned it on the pillow by her ear. "It certainly isn't going to happen that way if you don't stop touching me."

"But I like touching you," she countered, lifting up to kiss his chin. She'd been aiming for his lips, but with his chest pressed against hers, she couldn't lift up that high. "Kissing you." She could barely gain the breath she needed for speech as his body slid down hers. "I've been waiting a long time for this."

"Then let's not delay."

Further conversation became impossible as Gabriel kicked off his boxers and slid between her thighs. Olivia felt his erection against her skin and wiggled her hips to entice him to bring their bodies together in the way they both wanted. Her entire focus consisted of this powerful man and the ache only he could satisfy. Despite her inexperience, she knew exactly what she wanted. Gabriel inside her. She needed to be connected to him on that elemental level and she needed it now.

"Gabriel, please," she murmured, her body shuddering as his mouth slipped over her skin, licking, nibbling, kissing. He seemed determined to investigate every inch of her when there was only one place she wanted his attention focused. "Take me."

Her voice broke on the plea. But it had its effect. He kissed her one last time on the hollow beside her hip bone and settled the tip of his shaft at the entrance to her core. The feel of him there was so amazing. She lifted her hips and took him a little way in.

"We'll get there," he murmured, framing her face with his hands.

Surrendering to the ride was part of the excitement. Forcing him to move faster would get her to satisfaction quicker but wasn't the journey worth some patience?

"You're extremely tight." Capturing her lips in a hot, sizzling kiss, Gabriel flexed his hips forward, sliding into her a little deeper. "It will go easier the first time if you relax."

She was a mass of anticipation and tension. How the hell was she supposed to relax? Olivia gripped his wrists and focused on his expression. His rigid facial muscles and intense concentration told her that this slow loving was taking its toll on him, as well.

"I have no idea how to do that." The heavy throb in her womb grew more powerful as she held her breath and waited for him to join with her completely.

His low chuckle sounded near her ear.

"Breathe."

"I can't." Her words were garbled, starved for air.

His teeth nipped her throat and she gasped. Then he was sucking on the spot where he'd administered the love bite, his tongue laving the tender area. Her mouth fell open as an electric charge shot from where he'd placed his mouth to the place where he was claiming her in the most elemental way possible. Her body stretched as he rocked against her again, his movement driving him a little deeper into her.

The sensation was incredible. She focused on the joy of being filled by him and her muscles unwound. Relief swept through her and she gave herself over to wonder with a murmur.

"Or maybe I can."

"That's it," he coaxed, withdrawing with the same deliberate motion only to move into her again.

The sensation was incredible. She loved the way he filled her.

It took a moment of concentration before she shifted her hips into sync with his slow rhythm. Which was too slow as it turned out. He might have all the patience in the world, but she didn't. His gentleness wasn't getting him where she needed him most. So, as he began his next measured, torturous thrust into her body, she arched her back, drove her hips forward and sunk her nails into his tight rear, accepting all of him. They cried out in unison. If she hadn't been so shattered by the feel of him so deeply buried in her, Olivia might have giggled. Utterly possessed, she had no breath to laugh or speak.

Gabriel licked his lips and slowly his gaze refocused. The transformation of his features from rigid concentration to outright shock magnified the pleasure inside her.

"What happened to slow?" he murmured, fingertips grazing her cheeks with reverent gentleness.

Olivia's body had adjusted to his. A contented purr rumbled in her chest. She ran the soles of her feet down his calves and drifted her hands along his spine.

"You were taking too long."

"It's your first time," he grumbled. "I was trying to be gentle."

"What happens now?" Her inner muscles flexed as he rocked his hips against hers.

"Watch and see."

With those cryptic words, Olivia turned herself over to the dazzling display of fireworks in Gabriel's eyes as he began to move against her, gauging her every response. Then he thrust back inside her and pleasure began to build once more.

He captured her hips in his hands and helped her find his rhythm. To her astonishment her body caught fire. Pleasure radiated outward from her core, spreading in waves of sensual hunger that climbed higher and higher, reaching outward with an intensity that made her feel as if she was on the verge of splintering into a million pieces.

And then it began, the breaking. Yet this time, unlike the last, she had Gabriel with her, climbing beside her. She held on to him, glorying in his strength and the power of the pleasure he gave her.

Her breath caught as the sun exploded behind her eyelids. Ecstasy blasted through her, detonating with all the power of a volcano. She cried out and clung to Gabriel as his movements increased. Everything went dark for a second, then she heard her name on Gabriel's lips and he thrust one last time, shaking with the power of his orgasm, before collapsing on her.

Olivia tunneled one hand through his hair while her other unlocked from his shoulder. His chest heaved against her, as he dragged air into his lungs in great gulps. Their hearts thundered in unison, as matched in the aftermath as they'd been during their loving.

She scrambled for words, but nothing could describe her emotions at the moment. Instead, she settled for silence and let her fingers talk for her. She ran them soothingly across his skin, conveying her profound thanks.

"Are you okay?" Gabriel asked, rousing himself enough to slide out of her and roll onto his side.

The loss of him from her body hit her like a sledgehammer. The connection they'd had, now severed, made her realize just how intimate the act of making love was. For those few minutes, she'd not just taken him into her body, into her womb, but into her heart, as well. He'd possessed her body and soul.

"Never better," she replied, unable to mask the smile in her voice.

He gathered her close and dropped a chaste kiss above her brow. Beneath her palm, his heartbeat returned to normal.

"That makes two of us." His thumb moved against her shoulder in an absent fashion as if his mind was somewhere besides the two of them naked in this bed. "You're sure that wasn't too rough?"

"Since I have nothing to compare it to, I'm going to say it was just rough enough."

He stopped staring at the canopy overhead and sliced a sharp look her way. His mouth tightened for a second until he realized she was teasing him.

"I had hoped to initiate you in a more civilized manner."

"There's a civilized way to make love?" Despite her best intentions, she giggled. "Do tell." Lifting onto her elbow, she walked her fingers down his stomach. "Better yet, why don't you show me?"

Gabriel growled and captured her fingers in a tight grip, placing their clasped hands on his chest. "Behave."

"Or what?" She had no idea what demon had possessed her but suddenly she felt more free and alive than any time in her life. Keeping her virginity intact all these years had obviously created a powder keg of trouble. Like a genie in a bottle, once released, her sexuality was ready to cause as much mischief as possible before she stuffed it back in and replaced the cork. "You'll spank me?"

Gabriel's eyes widened at her outrageous suggestion, but temptation danced in their bronze depths. His pupils widened, a sure sign of sexual arousal, and his erection flared to life again.

And shockingly enough, she felt herself awakening, as well. What did this man do to her?

"You led me to believe you were cool and composed," he complained as she wiggled around until she got a thigh on either side of his hips. His erection prodded her from behind. He looked pained as she extricated her hand from his grasp and raked her nails down his chest and over his abdomen, smiling as his muscles twitched beneath her touch. "What's gotten into you?"

She leaned forward to grin at him. "You."

His hands bracketed her hips as she poised herself over his shaft and slowly lowered herself downward. Taking him deep, adjusting the angle to give herself the most pleasure, she watched his face contort with delight and his eyes glaze over.

When she sat on him, savoring the feel of him buried inside her once more, she watched his gaze come back into focus. He reached up to capture her breasts in his hands, kneading gently, pulling at her nipples while she rose off him, mimicking the slow way he'd tortured her.

For a while he let her control the action, and she appreciated the chance to learn how the feel of him sliding in and out of her could be different if she leaned forward or backward. She liked taking him deep until the tip of him nudged against her womb.

But her education would not be complete without a little tutoring, and Gabriel's patience couldn't last forever. His fingers bit into her hips, changing her cadence. He began to move powerfully, driving himself into her. The bite of her nails created half-moons in his shoulders as his hand slid between their bodies and touched the knot of nerves hidden in her hot wet lips. Sparks exploded behind her eyes as her body began to pulse with ever stronger pleasure. She threw her head back and her mouth fell open in a keening cry as pleasure spun through her like a cyclone.

Gabriel thrust into her, his pace frantic, his own mouth open to expel a groan of acute pleasure. Olivia watched him climax, watched him become completely hers. Panting, she trembled in the aftershocks of her orgasm, her inner muscles clenching around his shaft as he poured his seed inside her and she welcomed this essence of him she could keep.

For the past two hours, Gabriel had lain beside Olivia and listened to her deep regular breathing while his thoughts retraced the evening. As morning light began to come in through the windows, he rolled out of bed, moving carefully to avoid waking Olivia. While he dressed he kept his eyes off her to avoid succumbing to the temptation to return to bed and wake her. Again. A full-fledged grin engaged every muscle in Gabriel's face. He couldn't help it.

Making love with Olivia had demonstrated his life would be spectacularly entertaining from here on out.

As he exited her room, he wondered if she'd done it on purpose. Picked a fight with him that ended in spectacular lovemaking. It was something Marissa had done often enough. Sex with her had been mind-blowing, hot, passionate, animalistic. She'd scratched long welts on his back and marked his shoulders with love bites. She'd possessed him as much as he'd possessed her.

But although their sex had been out of this world, it had many times left him feeling empty. And in typical male fashion, he'd ignored the emotional vacuum because what did he care if his carnal needs were satisfied.

Then, last night, he'd discovered what he'd been missing all those years. Spectacular sex and a deep emotional connection that left him more than a little rattled. With her curious innocence and startling sensuality, Olivia had slipped beneath his skin as if she'd been there all along. As if she was the answer to a prayer he hadn't even realized he'd breathed.

He hadn't liked the sexual power Marissa had held in her delicate hands. He liked Olivia's ability to influence his emotions even less.

Which was why he was heading for his suite of rooms rather than face her in the moments before dawn.

An hour later, Gabriel found Stewart in the office on the first floor. His private secretary had a cup of coffee at his elbow and wore a troubled frown.

"You're up early," Gabriel commented, settling himself behind the intricately carved cherry desk.

"I think you might be interested in seeing this." Stewart extended a jewelry box in Gabriel's direction.

He frowned at it. "What is that?"

Stewart nudged his chin at the box. "When Lady Darcy's secretary delivered her message that she wasn't joining you for dinner, she gave me this. You left before I had a chance to open it."

With an impatient snort, Gabriel cracked open the box. The hairs on the back of his neck lifted as he stared at the contents.

"Where the hell did this come from?" he growled, staring in shocked dismay at the bracelet he'd given Marissa for their second anniversary. "Why did Olivia have it?"

Stewart shook his head. "I spoke with her secretary this morning and apparently it was waiting in her room when she got back from her fitting."

"No wonder she was so angry." He closed the box with a snap. "Ariana must have told her I'd bought this for Marissa."

"Who would have done this?" Stewart asked, refocusing Gabriel on the real trouble spot.

"Whoever it was wanted to create trouble between Olivia and me." Gabriel sat back and steepled his fingers.

"Someone could have entered her suite and left it for her. Staff is coming and going all the time."

"That means someone in the palace is playing a dangerous game." Gabriel poked at the box with a pen. "Time to give Christian a call. This sort of intrigue is right up his alley."

Seven

Finding Gabriel gone when she awoke didn't surprise Olivia. A quick glance at the clock told her it was past eight. He had probably been up for hours. She eased into a sitting position, taking inventory of every strained and aching part of her. Nothing a hot shower wouldn't cure.

When she stepped from the bathroom a short time later, she discovered a visitor. Gabriel sat beside a table laden with an array of breakfast offerings. With his long legs stretched out in front of him and his hands clasped around a steaming cup of coffee, he hadn't yet noticed her.

Olivia leaned her shoulder against the door frame and let her gaze drift over his strong features and muscular torso clad in a tailored midnight-blue suit, white shirt and shimmering burgundy silk tie. For the moment his powerful energy was banked. But Gabriel in a contemplative state was no less arresting than him fully engaged.

Some small sound, probably a dreamy sigh, alerted him to her presence. He straightened and came toward her, his movement fluid, and before she knew it, he'd wrapped her in a snug embrace and given her the lusty morning kiss she'd been hoping for when she'd first awakened.

Desire stirred at the firm press of his mouth against her. He tasted of coffee and raspberries. Olivia dipped her tongue in for a second taste, murmuring approval.

"Good morning," he said, breaking the kiss, but not

ceasing the slow advance of his hands up her spine. "I'm sorry I left without doing that earlier."

"Why didn't you wake me?" She snuggled her cheek against his chest, savoring the unsteady pace of his heart and the hoarse timbre of his voice.

"Because I would have wanted to pick up where we left off last night," he retorted, his voice soft and deep. "And the palace would have been fully awake by the time I left your room."

That wrenched a laugh out of her. "You don't think everyone knows what happened last night?" Her cheeks heated despite herself. She'd always known there would be no privacy for her in the palace, but facing his parents and siblings when she knew they'd be apprised of what had happened between them last night would take a little getting used to.

"Perhaps, but I'd prefer to at least give the appearance of propriety until we're married." Gabriel gave her a wry smile that enhanced the devilry in his eyes. "Are you hungry?"

Her hands snaked around his waist, to tug his crisp white shirt from his pants. "Starving."

With a deep, rumbling laugh he caught her wrists. "I meant for breakfast. We missed dinner last night."

She waited until he'd dusted a kiss across her knuckles before answering. "I'd quite forgotten about dinner."

His eyes glowed with fierce delight as he drew her toward the table and poured a cup of coffee. "I didn't know what you liked for breakfast so I ordered some of everything."

"Usually I have an egg-white omelet with mushrooms and spinach, but today I think I want pancakes with lots of syrup."

To her astonishment, Gabriel served her himself. Olivia found it quite difficult to concentrate on her delicious breakfast while he watched her through eyes that danced with fondness and desire.

"Aren't you eating?" she asked.

"I had something an hour ago." He glanced at his watch. "The girls are going for their first ride this morning. I thought we should go watch. I already checked with your secretary and she said you're available until ten."

Considering his busy schedule, Olivia was delighted that he'd made time for such an important event. "They'll be thrilled. I took them to the stables yesterday afternoon. They loved the ponies. I predict they'll be enthusiastic equestrians."

"I have something for you." He pulled a small box out of his pocket and set it on the table between them.

Olivia eyed the black velvet case on the crisp white linen and shook her head. "I don't want it." The memory of yesterday's gift had made her more blunt than polite.

Gabriel didn't look at all surprised or insulted by her refusal. "You don't know that until you open it."

More of his mistress's leftovers? Olivia heaved a sigh. "You really don't need to give me anything."

"I need to explain about the bracelet."

She did not want to hear about the wretched thing ever again. "There's nothing to explain. It was beautiful. It was rude of me not to accept something you put so much thought into."

Gabriel leaned back in his chair, his expression a mask. But his eyes glittered like sunlight on water. "I'm not certain whether to be appalled or delighted that you are such a skillful diplomat."

She kept her lashes down and her lips relaxed. All her life she'd been watched for any sign of reaction or weakness. She'd mastered her facial muscles well before her fourteenth birthday. And she'd needed to. Her stepmother had enjoyed poking her with emotional sticks. Any reaction was sure to displease Lord Darcy, who wanted nothing more than for his two girls to get on. He was fond of reminding the women that he loved them both. And wished with all his heart that they would get along.

"You are marrying me because of my diplomacy and public image."

"In part." Gabriel turned over her hand and set the box on her palm. "I'm also marrying you because of your impeccable breeding and the fact that ever since the day I met you, I haven't been able to stop thinking about you."

Stunned by his admission, she stared at Gabriel's gift, knowing no expensive bauble could compare to the gift of knowing he was smitten with her. "That's lovely of you to say."

"Now back to the bracelet. Do you know where it came from?"

His question confused her. "From you."

He shook his head. "This is what I selected for you."

"Then where did the bracelet come from?"

"That's what I'd like to know."

Relief swept through her. "Then you didn't give me Marissa's bracelet."

"No." He gave her a stern look. "And I'm a little bothered by the fact that you think I'd be so cruel."

Olivia opened her mouth but had no ready response. Since dancing with him at the Independence Day gala she'd become foolish and irrational where he was concerned. With her hormones overstimulated and her emotions swinging from one extreme to the other, she shouldn't be surprised her brain was producing nothing but gibberish.

"Someone in the palace with access to my room played a cruel joke on me."

"Whoever it is, I don't think they are playing. This is a very serious breach in security. One that I will address." The determination in his voice matched the steel in his expression. After a second his gaze softened. "Please open my gift."

Olivia did as she was told.

Unlike the previous evening's trendy, emerald bracelet, this necklace was exactly something she would have chosen for herself. Olivia touched her fingertip to the large teardrop-shaped aquamarine, set into a frame of diamond-lined branches and suspended from a chain of faceted aquamarine beads and diamond-encrusted platinum balls. Gabriel had picked out the perfect, unique gift.

"The necklace belonged to my great-aunt Ginnie. Her husband gave it to her as an engagement present. I believe it came from his mother who received it as her engagement present."

"I love it." And she did. More than any million-dollar diamond necklace he could have found in the treasury. It represented tradition and love. And it demonstrated a sentimental side she would never have guessed Gabriel possessed. Feeling bold, she picked up the necklace and sat down on her fiancé's lap. "Can you help me put it on?"

She lifted her hair off her neck and held still while his knuckles brushed her nape. The casual touch sent shivers spiraling along her nerve endings. As the drop settled against her skin, she turned and planted a sweet kiss on Gabriel's cheek.

"Is that the best you can do?" he questioned, laughter in his voice.

Veiling her eyes with her lashes, she peered at him. "If I do much better we run the risk of not leaving this room in time to take Bethany and Karina for their first ride."

His response was to capture her lips in a sizzling kiss. Olivia sagged against him, surrendering to the firestorm of desire that had not burned out even after last night's lovemaking. She groaned beneath his lips as his hand found her breast, thumb coaxing her nipple to a hard point.

With a low growl, he broke off the kiss. "Perhaps you were right to be cautious." And with that, he stood with her in his arms and carried her to the bed.

In the end, they were in time to watch the twins circle the ring on the docile, well-mannered ponies, each led by an attentive groom. Although both were equally delighted by the ride, their individual personalities shone through. Bethany chattered incessantly as she rode, her every thought voiced. Karina was more circumspect and her seat was more natural. Of the two, Gabriel suspected she'd be the better rider.

Soon the twins' first riding lesson was done, leaving Gabriel free to turn his thoughts to the woman beside him and all that had transpired in the past twelve hours.

Since discovering last night how swiftly Olivia became aroused, he'd taken full advantage of her ardent responses and made love to her with fierce passion. Already his lust for her was dangerously close to uncontrollable. Telling himself making love to Olivia was a novelty that would soon wear off wasn't cooling his ardor one bit. Even now, as he watched her smile as her gaze followed the twins, he felt heat rise in his blood.

It shocked him to realize that he'd happily forgo the rest of his appointments to spend the time alone with Olivia in her suite. This was how he'd been with Marissa. Preoccupied. Distracted. Obsessed.

Then again, it was early in their relationship. The time of exploration when all things were fascinating and new. Their lust would eventually burn itself out and they could settle into companionable monotony. But even as he entertained this possibility his instincts rejected it. More than his blood hummed when she was near. This was a feeling he'd never known before. Besides being beautiful, Olivia was intelligent and caring. He'd been right the first time he'd pronounced her perfect. But he'd underestimated how deep that flawlessness went.

"Gabriel?" Olivia said, returning him to the here and now. "I was just explaining to Bethany and Karina that we can't have dinner with them tonight."

"Because we are…" He had no idea what was scheduled that evening. How was that possible? He usually knew his itinerary backward and forward.

"Going to the ballet," Olivia prompted.

"That's it." He smiled at her.

"But perhaps we could visit before we leave to read you one quick bedtime story."

"That we can do."

The twins' chorus of happiness sent a bird winging off through the trees from a few feet away.

"I think it's time to head back to the palace," Olivia said, shaking her head as the girls began to protest. "Your father has work to do."

Gabriel was impressed how well she managed the toddlers. The twins were darling but rambunctious. Marissa had done a fine job of blending discipline with love for they seemed to take direction well and had none of the fits of temper he had grown accustomed to with their mother. Despite losing Marissa recently, they were adjusting nicely to life in the palace. Of course, they had each other, something he could relate to with two brothers of his own. Sometimes it had seemed as if it was him, Nic and Christian against the world when in truth it was probably more reasonable to say it had been the three of them against their parents.

After leaving the twins in the hands of two young maids, Gabriel walked Olivia to her meeting with the wedding planner and bussed her cheek in a chaste kiss goodbye. He had fifteen minutes before his first meeting of the day and went in search of Christian.

His brother was nowhere near the palace. Christian had an office in the city that he usually preferred to work out of, claiming fewer distractions. Gabriel suspected he liked working without the king's or queen's "subtle" influence. With two brothers ahead of him for the throne, Christian had always enjoyed a lot of freedom. So had Nic. The middle brother didn't even live in Sherdana. He'd gotten his education in the States and resided in California while he pursued his dream of privatizing space travel.

Gabriel envied them both.

And he wouldn't trade places with, either. He'd been born to rule and had never wished to do anything else. But being king came with a price. He belonged to the people of Sherdana and owed it to them to do what was best for the country, even at the expense of his own desires. Breaking off his relationship with Marissa was only one of many sacrifices he'd made for Sherdana, but it had been his hardest and most painful.

It was why he was marrying a woman he admired instead of one he loved. And yet, hadn't last night and this morning proved that life with Olivia at his side would be the furthest thing from hardship?

Grinning, Gabriel headed into his father's office where the energy minister had come for a briefing.

Olivia yawned behind her hand as she surveyed Noelle's drawings for the twins' dresses for the wedding. It was almost midnight. She'd just returned from another event, this one raising money for an arts program for underprivileged children.

She wasn't insensible to the irony that what she intended to pay for these two dresses could probably fund the program for a year.

Behind her the door to her suite opened and closed. Her skin prickled in anticipation as muted footsteps advanced toward her. The faint scent of Gabriel's aftershave tickled her nose a second before his hands soothed along her shoulders.

"Waiting up for me?"

Gabriel placed a kiss on her neck, his lips sliding into a particularly sensitive spot that made her tremble.

Was it possible that less than a week ago their every private encounter had been stilted and awkward? Now she spent her days as a tightly wound spring of sexual anticipation and her nights in Gabriel's arms soaring toward the stars.

"Of course," she answered, setting aside the sketches and getting to her feet. She'd already dressed for bed in her favorite silk pajamas. They covered her from neck to toe. Not exactly seductive, but Gabriel never seemed to care.

"I'm leaving early in the morning," he explained, pulling her into his arms and dropping a sweet kiss on her lips. "And I will be gone for four days. I wanted a private moment with you before I left."

Four long days. And nights. She'd gotten accustomed to cuddling against his side, her cheek on his bare chest, his heartbeat lulling her to sleep.

She adored his intensity—making love with Gabriel was like being consumed by the sun—but these moments of stillness had their own rewards.

"Just a moment?" She tipped her head to grant him better access to her neck and ran her nails along his nape the way he liked.

"Did I mention I'm leaving very early in the morning?" Tender mockery filled his voice. He nudged his hips into her, letting her feel his erection. She smiled, no less turned on despite wanting to do nothing more than stretch out on her mattress and sleep for twelve hours.

"Of course," she murmured. "I just thought that perhaps you could give me a few minutes to say goodbye properly."

"Just a few minutes?"

Olivia's bones turned to water as he drew his tongue along her lower lip, tasting, but not taking. With his hands warm and strong on her lower back, she leaned into his powerful chest and savored the tantalizing slide of his mouth against hers.

"Take as many as you need."

She'd grown accustomed to sharing her bed with him and hated the thought of sleeping alone these next four nights. Every morning, after he woke her with kisses and made love to her in the soft light before day, she fell back to sleep wondering if once they were married, once she became pregnant, if he would share her bed every night. She already knew that a suite of rooms was being prepared for them in the family wing. They would each have their own space. Their own beds after the wedding. That wasn't what she wanted.

Olivia wasn't surprised when Gabriel swept her off her feet and carried her to the bed. The chemistry between them had skyrocketed in the days since they'd first made love. With their clothes scattered across the mattress, Olivia clutched at Gabriel as he brought her to orgasm twice before sliding into her. Being filled by him was a pleasure all its own and Olivia wrapped her thighs around his hips and held him close while he thrust into her.

He stayed for several hours, his large hands moving with such gentleness up and down her spine. Snuggled against his chest, with their legs intertwined, Olivia let herself drift. When she awoke several hours later, Gabriel was gone and she was already lonely.

Exhausted, but restless, Olivia left the bed and slipped into a robe. Her suite faced the gardens behind the palace so she had no hope of catching a final glimpse of Gabriel, but she opened the French door that led to the terrace and wandered across to the railing. At night the garden was lit up like a magical fairy tale, but dawn was approaching and the garden had gone dark. A cool breeze carried the scent of roses to her. Olivia leaned her arms on the cool stone. Vivid in her thoughts was the night Gabriel had found her out here and demonstrated that resisting him was a pointless exercise.

And now she knew it had been all along. When she'd agreed to marry him, she'd fooled herself into believing that sexual desire and mild affection would make her happy. After several nights in his arms she'd completely fallen under his spell. It was as if all her life she'd been moving toward this man and this moment.

Recognizing that her motivation for marrying Gabriel had changed, she had to ask herself if she was no longer concerned whether one day she'd become a queen...what did she really want?

Love.

The thought made her knees weak. Olivia braced herself against the stone railing. Deflated, she stared at her hands. At the engagement ring sparkling on her finger.

She couldn't be falling in love with Gabriel. He certainly wasn't falling in love with her.

This was an arranged marriage. A practical union for the good of his country. A sensible bargain that would lead to stability and children. She hadn't expected to fall madly in love with her husband or be deliriously happy. She expected to be content. To feel fulfilled as a mother and someday as a queen.

Sexual satisfaction hadn't entered into her plans—not until Gabriel had kissed her.

Olivia turned away from the softly lit garden and returned to her suite. As she closed and locked the glass door, her gaze fell on her desk and the locked drawer where she'd placed copies of important paperwork, including a file with some of her medical information. Had those scratches always marred the lock's brass surface? The idea that someone in the palace could have tried to break into her desk was ridiculous. And then she recalled the night the twins arrived. There'd been a maid at her dresser in the middle of the night. When nothing was missing she'd seen no reason to pursue it.

A few hours later, when Libby entered the suite, Olivia was still seated at the desk. She'd opened the locked drawer and hadn't found anything disturbed, but with the twins' arrival at the palace having been leaked to the press and the mysterious appearance of Marissa's bracelet, Olivia had checked each page of her thick file to make sure it was intact.

"Why are you looking through your papers?"

"I might be mistaken, but I thought I spotted fresh scratches on the lock and wanted to make sure my medical file hadn't been rifled." Olivia glanced up when Libby didn't immediately comment. "What's wrong?"

"Prince Christian is systematically interviewing the staff about the leaks to the press."

A chill chased across Olivia's skin. "He thinks someone inside the palace is providing information?" She remembered the photos of Gabriel and Marissa. Those hadn't been paparazzi shots. They had been taken among friends.

Olivia touched the lock again, wishing she could determine if the scratches were recent. If someone had gotten their hands on her medical records it could have catastrophic results. "Keep me updated on the investigation," she said, "and see if you can find a more secure place for these."

Gabriel was having a hard time keeping his mind on today's biotech plant tour. For the past several days he'd been touring manufacturing plants in Switzerland and Belgium in search of other businesses that would be interested in moving their operations to Sherdana. He probably should have sent Christian to do this. His brother had made a significant amount of money investing in up-and-coming technology. Christian would have been interested in the product lines and the way the manufacturing facilities were organized. Gabriel was finding it as dry as overdone toast.

That's probably how both his brothers felt about what went into the running of the country. These days, they had little in common. It often amazed Gabriel that three people could share a womb for nine months, communicate among themselves in their own language until they were teenagers and participate in a thousand childhood adventures together yet be so completely different in their talents and interests as they entered their twenties.

Nevertheless, this trip couldn't have come at a better time. The past few nights with Olivia had been some of the most passion-filled of his life. She'd slipped effortlessly beneath his defenses with her eager sensuality and curious nature. He'd become obsessed with the soft drag of her lips across his skin and the wicked suggestions she whispered in his ear as he entered her.

His constant craving for her company warned him he was fast losing touch with why he was marrying her. Cool, sophisticated elegance and a warm heart. Not feverish kisses and blazing orgasms.

Gabriel cleared his throat and tugged at his collar as the head of the factory droned on. He definitely needed some space from her. Unfortunately, the distance wasn't having the effect he'd hoped for. Being apart was supposed to cool him off. That was what he'd anticipated, but that wasn't the result.

He daydreamed about her at the oddest moments. Him. Daydreaming. Like some infatuated fool. He'd never expected her to preoccupy him in this way. She was supposed to be a sensible mate, an able partner in governing the country, not a hellcat in bed.

Hope.

The tattoo drove him crazy. Its placement. Its message.

It awakened him to possibilities. He wanted to throw sensible out the window and take chances. Because of Olivia he wanted to shake up the established way of doing things. She'd awakened his restless spirit that he'd believed he'd conquered after ending things with Marissa.

Every day he was finding out that Olivia was more than he'd expected.

And he'd be a fool not to worry about the power she now had over him. Yet he was helpless to stop what was developing between them. The best he could hope for was to slow things down until he shaped the relationship into something he was comfortable with.

But was *comfortable* going to make him happy in the long run? Was he really going to shortchange his future all for the sake of feeling safe and in control?

A few days after Gabriel left on his trip, Olivia was scheduled to have a private lunch with the queen. Ten minutes before the appointment, she slipped pearl earrings into place and stepped in front of the mirror to assess her appearance. She'd chosen a sleeveless pink dress edged in white with a narrow white belt to highlight her waist, and accessorized with a pair of floral pumps. The feminine ensemble required a soft hairstyle so she'd left her hair down and coaxed out the natural wave with a light blowout.

This morning she'd awakened to some discomfort in her lower abdomen and wasn't feeling on top of her game, but wasn't about to cancel on the queen.

Drawing a fortifying breath, she entered the private dining room that only the immediate royal family used. Pale blue had been chosen for the chairs as well as the curtains framing the large windows. It was the only splash of color in a room otherwise dominated by white walls and lavish plasterwork painted gold. More intimate than many of the other rooms on the first floor, it nevertheless didn't allow her to forget that this was a palace.

"You look lovely," the queen said as she breezed into the room. She wore a classic suit of dusty lavender and a stunning choker of pale round Tahitian pearls. Noticing Olivia's interest, she touched the necklace. "An anniversary gift from the king," the queen explained, her smile both fond and sensual.

"It's beautiful."

"Matteo has exceptionally good taste."

The queen gestured toward the dining table, capable of seating twelve, but set for two. As the two women sat down, a maid set a glass of soda on the table before the queen.

"Diet cola," she, sipping the fizzy drink with pleasure. "I got a taste for it when we visited the States two decades ago. It's my indulgence."

Olivia nodded in understanding. She wasn't much of a soda drinker herself, but she understood how someone could come to crave a particular item. Like a tall, bronze-eyed prince for example.

The servers placed plates of salad in front of the two women and the queen launched a barrage of questions to determine what Olivia knew about Sherdana's current political climate and their economic issues. Although Olivia had been expecting to discuss the wedding preparations, she was just as happy to share what she knew about the country she would soon call her own.

"Does my son know how bright you are?" the queen asked, her expression thoughtful as the maids cleared the main course and served dessert. She frowned at the plate in front of her and sighed. "Oh, dear. The chef is experimenting again."

Olivia stared at the oddest fruit she'd ever seen. About

the size of her fist with a leathery hot-pink skin, it had been sliced in half to reveal white flesh dotted with tiny black seeds. A hollow had been carved out of the center and filled with yogurt and sliced strawberries.

"Dragon fruit," the queen explained. "And from what I understand quite delicious."

Olivia took her first bite and was surprised at the wonderfully sweet flavor. It had a texture like a kiwi with the seeds adding a little crunch to each bite.

"You look pale." The queen pointed at Olivia with her spoon. "I expect you'll get more rest with my son away."

Olivia's entire body flushed hot. The queen had just insinuated that she knew where Gabriel had been spending his nights.

"Oh, don't look so mortified," the queen continued. "You are to be married and my son was determined to have a short engagement. Besides, there are no secrets in the palace."

"No, I suppose there are not." Olivia knew better than to think her nights with Gabriel were something between just the two of them. She'd grown up surrounded by servants who knew most everything about her daily habits.

"How are the twins' dresses coming for the wedding?" The queen had taken a few days to approve the idea of Bethany and Karina being a part of the ceremony, but Gabriel had at last persuaded her.

"They should be finished later this week. The lace Noelle has chosen is beautiful. I think you'll be pleased."

"Noelle is very talented. You will all look beautiful." The queen nodded in satisfaction. "I must say, you've accepted this situation with Gabriel's children much better than most women would in your position."

"It's hard to imagine anyone not adoring those precious two," Olivia admitted, but she understood what the queen was getting at. "I love children. Helping to make their lives better is the foundation for all my charity work. I would be a wretched person and a hypocrite if I turned my back on Bethany and Karina because of who their mother was." And what Marissa had meant to Gabriel.

"They certainly have taken to you," the queen said. "And you seem to have everything it takes to be an excellent mother."

"Thank you."

The queen's praise should have allowed Olivia to relax, but the tick of her biological clock sounded loud in her ears.

Eight

"How was the trip?" Christian asked as he and Gabriel crossed the tarmac toward the waiting limo. "I hope you brought me a present."

"Naturally." Gabriel hoisted his briefcase and deposited it in his brother's hands. "It's filled with all sort of things I'm sure you'll find vastly interesting."

"Unlike you?"

"Technology is more your and Nic's thing." Gabriel was aware that the trip had been less productive than he'd hoped. Mostly because he'd had a hard time concentrating. Thoughts of Olivia had intruded with a frequency he'd found troubling. "You probably should have gone instead of me, but it was something I needed to do. I want to encourage more technology firms to move to Sherdana. The best way for me to do that is to speak to companies that might be looking at expansion."

"I'll bet you hated it."

Gabriel shot Christian a quelling look. "I can't expect to enjoy every aspect of my position. Some things must be done no matter how painful. This was one of them."

"Is your future wife another?"

This time Christian laughed out loud at his brother's sharp look.

"How I feel about my future bride is none of your business."

"Come on, you've got to be a lot happier about having to get married these days. From what I hear, you two have been acting like a couple kids in love."

Gabriel growled in displeasure, but couldn't ignore the electric charge that surged through him at the mere thought of seeing Olivia again and feeling her soft lips yield beneath his. Each of the past four nights he'd gone to bed alone and found himself unable to sleep. Plagued by memories of Olivia's smiles and her sassy sensuality, he'd lain with his hands behind his head, staring up at the blank ceiling and doing his best to ignore his erection.

Cold showers had become his 2:00 a.m. ritual. How had she bewitched him in such a short time?

"Neither one of us is in love," Gabriel muttered. "But I won't deny we're compatible." He leveled a hard gaze at his brother, warning him to drop the matter.

"Not in love?" Christian cocked his head. "Maybe you're not. But are you sure about her?"

Christian's question roused a memory of the last evening before his trip. He'd almost succumbed to Olivia's plea to spend the night. She'd seemed so vulnerable, her characteristic confidence lacking. But that didn't mean she was in love with him.

"Ridiculous," he said. "We've only spent a couple weeks in each other's company."

"You don't believe in love at first sight?"

Gabriel regarded his brother's serious expression with curiosity. "Do you?"

"Absolutely."

"Is that why you do your best to chase every woman away who gets too close?" Gabriel wondered if his brother was taunting him or if he was offering Gabriel a rare glimpse into his psyche. "Have none of them made you feel as if you were clobbered by something beyond your understanding or control?"

Something flared in Christian's gaze but was quickly gone. His mocking smile returned. "Who wants to settle down with one woman when there's a banquet of lovelies to sample?"

"One of these days someone will appeal to your palate and you'll find that you can't get enough of that particular delicacy."

"Is that what happened to you?"

"I'm getting married because I have to." Gabriel was well aware that he'd dodged the question and not with any finesse.

Christian's eyes narrowed. "And if you didn't have to?"

"Since that's never been an option, I've never really thought about it."

And he didn't want to think about it now because it opened old wounds. Would he have stayed with Marissa if marriage to her had been possible? Had he loved her or had he inflated his feelings for her because circumstances made it impossible for them to have a future?

"Well, I certainly stirred you up," Christian taunted.

"Wasn't that your intention?" Gabriel countered, staring past the hedge that bordered the driveway to the palace. For a moment he glimpsed a pair of ponies and the two little girls riding them. Despite his tumultuous thoughts, he couldn't help but feel joy at the appearance of his daughters and feel sorry for Christian. His cynical attitude would undoubtedly prevent him from experiencing the wonder of holding his own children in his arms and feeling their enthusiastic kisses all over his cheek.

"God," Christian exclaimed, "you are smitten."

"I caught a glimpse of my angels out riding."

Christian snorted. "They're not exactly angels. In fact, they've been turning the palace upside down with their version of hide-and-seek, which entails them finding some tiny nook and not coming out until every servant is called upon to look for them. It's been worse these last few days with Olivia feeling unwell."

Gabriel frowned. "What did you say about Olivia? She's ill?"

"Didn't you know?"

"I spoke with her last night. She said nothing." Gabriel rubbed at the back of his neck. "How bad is it?"

"I don't know. She hasn't been out of her suite for the last two days."

"Has she been in bed that whole time?"

"I don't know," Christian sounded amused. "But if you'd hinted that you'd like me to check on your English flower in her bedroom, you should have said something."

Gabriel didn't even look at his brother as he exited the car and strode into the palace. Tension rode his shoulders as he entered the foyer, barely hearing the greetings from the staff on duty. Why hadn't Olivia told him she wasn't doing well? He took the stairs two at a time and turned in the direction of his fiancée's suite. His knock was answered by a maid.

"I'm here to see Lady Darcy," he told her, his scowl compelling the young woman to step back.

Three women occupied the room. Olivia sat on the couch with her feet up, her back to him while Ariana sat opposite her facing the door. Olivia's private secretary was by the desk. His sister's lilting laugh broke off as he entered.

"Good afternoon, ladies." He forced himself to approach Ariana first. His sister looked splendid as always in an evening-blue dress. The color flattered her golden skin and dark brown hair. She wore a simple gold bangle at her wrist and gold hoop earrings.

"Welcome back, Gabriel," she said, standing as he drew near and making her cheek available for a kiss.

"We missed you," Olivia echoed, turning to gaze up at

him. Her normally pale complexion lacked its customary healthy glow and there were shadows purpling the skin beneath her eyes.

Concern flared. He sat beside her on the sofa and touched her cheek with his fingertips. "Last night on the phone, why didn't you tell me you've been ill?"

"It's nothing."

"You're too pale. I demand to know what's wrong."

Olivia sighed and cast her gaze toward Ariana. Her eyes widened, causing Gabriel to turn his head. Ariana had vanished. The door to the bedroom was shut. They were alone.

Gabriel refocused on Olivia. "Answer me," he growled.

Red patches appeared on her formerly dull cheeks. "I've been having a particularly difficult period," she murmured.

Relief flooded him. She was embarrassed to discuss her body's natural process? Was that why she'd kept silent the night before? Amused, Gabriel dipped a finger beneath her chin and raised it.

"I'm going to be your husband. You better prepare to discuss all sorts of things like this with me."

"Be careful or you may live to regret those words," she muttered, but her lips were soft and eager beneath his. "Welcome home."

An endearment hung between them, unspoken. She'd promised not to call him Prince Gabriel or Your Highness as they made love, but she had yet to find a pet name for him. What would it be? Darling? Dearest? Sweetheart? My love?

"Did you have a successful trip?" she asked.

"It was very long." He leaned forward and kissed her neck below her ear, smiling as she trembled. "And lonely."

She framed his face with her hands. "I missed you so much. In fact—"

A knock sounded on the door, interrupting her. Heaving

a weary sigh, Gabriel kissed Olivia on the nose and then raised his voice to be heard in the hall. "Come."

Stewart poked his head around the door. "The king wondered if you'd gotten lost on your way to the meeting with the prime minister."

Gabriel stood and bent over Olivia's hand. "Duty calls."

"Of course." The bright smile she gave him didn't quite reach her eyes. "Perhaps we can have dinner together?"

Regret pinched him. "I'm afraid I can't tonight. I already have an appointment."

"Of course."

He'd grown familiar with the micro expressions that belied her thoughts and could see she was disappointed. He hated being the one who robbed her eyes of their sparkle, and the intensity of his desire to see her smile caught him off guard. Falling in love with his fiancée wasn't what he'd had in mind when he decided to marry Olivia.

"I'll stop back to check on you later," he said.

Her gaze clung to his face. "I'll be waiting."

The morning after Gabriel returned from his business trip, Olivia caught herself smiling almost as often as she yawned. True to his word, he'd returned after his dinner to check on her and they'd snuggled on the sofa until almost three in the morning while Olivia filled him in on the twins and he spoke of what he'd seen in Switzerland and Belgium.

In addition to talking, there'd been a fair amount of kissing, as well. Lighthearted, romantic kisses that left Olivia breathless and giddy. He'd treated her with tender patience, not once letting passion get the better of him. Olivia had found his control both comforting and frustrating. Four days without him had aroused her appetite for his hands roaming over her skin and she cursed her cycle's timing.

On the other hand, there would be nothing to get in the

way of their magical wedding night. Unless there wasn't going to be a wedding.

This was her first period since discontinuing the birth control pills that regulated her cycle. At first she'd been down because as amazing as her nights with Gabriel had been, she hadn't gotten pregnant. Soon, however, she began to worry as old, familiar symptoms appeared. Assuring herself everything was going to be fine became harder each day as her period stretched out. For the past two days fear had begun to sink deep into bone and sinew. She began to confront the very real possibility that her surgery might not have cleared up her problem. She had to face that getting and staying pregnant might be more difficult than she'd assumed.

Then, after seeing Gabriel yesterday, it became clear what she had to do. She needed to tell him the truth. Despite the connection they shared, she wasn't sure how he was going to react to her news. She could only hope he would act like his father and work with her to solve any issues that came up.

"Olivia?"

A soft voice roused her. With the paparazzi hungry for their first glimpse of Gabriel's daughters, Olivia had requested that Noelle bring their flower-girl dresses to the palace to be fitted. Blinking, she refocused on the slim, dark-haired woman.

"Sorry, Noelle. With the wedding two weeks away my mind tends to jump around a great deal these days. What were you saying?"

"I asked if you wanted me to bring your dress here next week for the final fitting rather than have you come to my shop."

"It would help me if you brought the dress by. I'm drowning in wedding preparations and that would save me time."

"I'd be happy to."

A moment later the twins appeared in their new finery. They looked like angels in their matching sleeveless white dresses with full lace skirts and wide satin sashes in pale yellow. Noelle's assistant had pinned up their hair and attached wreaths wrapped in pale yellow ribbons.

"These are merely to demonstrate one possible look for the girls," Noelle explained. "If you like it, I'm sure the florist could create beautiful wreaths with yellow roses."

"The dresses are perfect," Olivia breathed. "Thank you so much for making them on such short notice."

"I'm happy you like them."

While Noelle and her assistant made little adjustments to the dresses, Olivia distracted Bethany and Karina by explaining to them what their role in the wedding would be. They seemed to understand the seriousness of the event because they listened to her with wide eyes and their full attention.

An hour later, Noelle had left, taking the dresses with her, and Olivia was reading the twins a story when the door to her suite swung open without warning. Startled, Olivia swiveled on the sofa to face a very unhappy Gabriel.

"What's wrong?"

"It's time for the twins to head back to the nursery," he answered, his voice level and cool as he gestured to the nanny who jumped to her feet. "I think it's time for their lunch."

Olivia set the book aside and got to her feet to urge the girls over to their father for a kiss and a hug. His manner softened for them, but a minute later they were gone and Gabriel was back to scowling.

"Is it true?" he demanded.

Her stomach twisted at the hard suspicion in his eyes. "Is what true?"

"That you're infertile?"

Of all the things that had raced through her mind, this was the last thing she'd expected. How had he found out? Libby was the only person who knew about her condition and Olivia knew her private secretary would never betray her.

"Where did you hear that?"

He stalked across the room toward the television and snatched up the remote. Dread filled Olivia as he cued the power button. She'd not imagined he could look so angry.

"Sources inside the palace confirm that the future princess has little to no chance of producing an heir for Sherdana's throne. With her medical condition you have to wonder what the prince was thinking to propose."

The words blaring from the television were so horrifying that Olivia would have crumpled to the floor at his feet if Gabriel hadn't seized her arms in a bruising grip.

His gaze bore into hers. "Tell me the truth."

"I had a condition," she began, and at his dark scowl, rushed on. "But I had surgery to correct the problem. I should be able to get pregnant." But after these past few days and the return of her old symptoms, her confidence had waned.

"Can you or can't you?"

"Six months ago when you proposed I thought I could. At this moment I honestly don't know."

"You should have told me." He set her free as if the touch of her was distasteful. "Did you think you could keep this a secret forever?"

"I really didn't think it was going to be a problem." Olivia clasped her hands to keep them from shaking and looked up at Sherdana's crown prince, who stood there like a granite statue. Little about his current demeanor encouraged hope that he might listen to her with a rational ear. "I would never have agreed to marry you if I believed I couldn't have children."

"But your doctor warned you the chances were slim." It wasn't a question.

She didn't ask him how he knew that. The reporter on the television was divulging her detailed medical records. Her privacy had been violated and yet she was being treated like a villain.

"He never said slim. He said there was a good chance I could get pregnant, but to do so I had to stop taking the pill and he wasn't sure how my body would react since I've been on it almost ten years."

"But you were a virgin. I can attest to that. Why were you on birth control?"

"I had severe cramps and bleeding. It helps control those problems." Olivia wrapped her arms around herself. "I quit taking the birth control before I left London. I wanted to get pregnant as soon as possible. Provide you with your heir. I knew that's what you all would expect."

Gabriel's expression didn't change, but his lips tightened briefly. "We expected you to be truthful, as well."

She flinched at his sharp words.

"I intended to tell you tonight. I haven't felt right these last few days and thought I needed to discuss the situation with you."

"I need an heir, Olivia." His harsh tone softened.

"I understand completely." Their marriage was an arrangement, an exchange of her hand in marriage for her father's business. But she was also expected to be a mother. "I never would've agreed to marry you knowing I might not be able to have children."

He needed to marry someone who could provide the next generation of Alessandros. At the moment she wasn't completely convinced she could do that.

A sharp pain lanced through her and she winced. Her cramps had been a dull ache all through the morning, but now they gained in strength.

"Are you okay?"

She shook her head. "It's been a hectic morning and I've done too much. I should probably take something and lie down for a while. Can we continue later this afternoon?"

She barely waited for his agreement before heading toward the bathroom and the bottle of pain medication she hadn't needed earlier in the day. She shut the bathroom door, hoping that Gabriel wouldn't come to check on her, and braced her hands on the vanity top. The woman in the mirror had dark circles beneath her eyes and white around her mouth.

The pain in her body was vivid and icy, very unlike her usual cramps. The difference scared her.

Forcing herself to take deep, even breaths, she fought back nausea and swallowed her medication. Within minutes, the sharp edges came off the ache in her pelvis and she was able to return to the bedroom. There she found Libby waiting for her with the queen. Helpless tears filled Olivia's eyes. She blinked them away.

"Have you tried pineapple juice?"

The queen's suggestion confused Olivia. "No."

"There's something in it that will help with your cramps."

Olivia clasped her hands as her stomach flipped sickeningly. Why was the queen being nice, given the news?

"Thank you. I'll try pineapple juice."

"You aren't the first woman in this palace to grapple with reproductive issues. I was young when I came to marry the king and eager to give him the heir he needed. Unlike Gabriel, Matteo had no male siblings to take over the throne if something happened to him."

"You had trouble getting pregnant?"

"There's a good reason why Gabriel has two brothers so close in age." The queen gave a fond smile. "I wasn't able to get pregnant without help. We did in vitro fertilization twice before the procedure was successful. Gabriel, Nicolas and Christian are the result."

"And Ariana?" The princess was six years younger than her brothers, close to Olivia's own age.

"My miracle baby."

Olivia liked the sound of that. She hoped her own miracle baby was on the horizon. Because the way she felt at the moment, a miracle might be exactly what she needed.

"Do you love my son?"

She rolled the engagement ring around and around on her finger. "Yes."

"Good, then you'll do what's best for him."

And leaving Olivia to ponder what that was, the queen took her leave.

When the door opened a short time later, Olivia looked up, expecting Libby, and saw a maid instead. "I really don't need anything right now. Perhaps you could check back in later this evening."

"I thought you'd like me to pack your things. I'm sure you'll be heading back to England now that the prince knows you can't have children."

The woman's snide tone wasn't at all what Olivia was expecting and she sat up straighter, adrenaline coursing through her veins. Of average height and appearance with brown hair and hazel eyes, the woman looked like any of a dozen palace maids. But there was a frantic energy to her movement that made Olivia apprehensive.

"Don't be ridiculous," she said, feeling at a disadvantage as the maid stalked toward her. "I'm not leaving."

Olivia pushed to her feet. The sudden movement sent pain stabbing through her. She swayed and caught the back of the chair. Her breath came in labored gasps. Something was very wrong.

"Of course you are." The woman's hazel eyes burned

with a crazy zeal. "The prince won't marry you now that he knows you're damaged."

"That's for him to decide." It was hard to keep her mind on the conversation when it felt as if hot pokers were being driven into her lower abdomen. "Get out."

"What makes you think you can order me around?" the woman spat. "Because you have a title and your father has money?"

Step by deliberate step, Olivia backed away from the maid's furious outburst. It was then that she recognized the woman's face. She'd been the one who'd been searching the desk the night the twins arrived.

"Who are you?" she asked.

"My sister was twice the woman you could ever hope to be."

The woman made as if to rush at her and Olivia stumbled backward.

"Marissa was your sister?" Impossible. This woman was as plain and dull as Marissa had been beautiful and vibrant.

"My younger sister. She was beautiful and full of life. Or she was until Prince Gabriel destroyed her."

"What do you mean?"

Olivia knew she had to keep the woman talking. Somewhere behind her was the bathroom with a solid door and a lock. She just needed to get there.

"In the months following her trip to visit him in Venice, she grew more and more depressed. She couldn't live with the fact that he wanted nothing more to do with her." The sister glared at Olivia as if she'd been the cause of Marissa's heartache.

"I'm sorry your sister was upset—"

"Upset?" The woman practically spat the word. "She wasn't upset. She was devastated. Devastated enough to try to kill herself. I was the one who found her bleeding to death. She'd slit her wrists. It was at the hospital that she found out she was pregnant. She loved her girls. They were everything to her."

Olivia reached her hand back and found the bathroom door frame. "Bethany and Karina are wonderful."

"He doesn't deserve them. He doesn't deserve to be happy. And now he won't because you can't have children. He won't want you anymore." Marissa's sister was shouting now, her voice rising in unbalanced hysteria.

Another wave of pain made Olivia double over. She backed into the bathroom and clawed at the door. Blackness pushed at the edges of her vision. By feel alone she shut the door and slid the lock into place. The door rattled as Marissa's sister beat against it in fury and Olivia staggered back.

With her strength failing, Olivia slid to the floor and set her back against the vanity, hoping that the door would hold. Hoping that someone would come find her. Hoping that Marissa's sister was wrong about Gabriel.

Nine

Gabriel leaned forward in the saddle and urged his stallion to greater speed. Wind lashed at his face, and he focused on the thrum of hoofbeats filling his ears to slow his racing mind. He'd gone for a ride after leaving Olivia because he needed to sort through the conflict raging in him.

Although the powerful Warmblood had stamina enough for a longer run, Gabriel slowed him to a walk after only a mile. He passed the lake where he and his brothers had swum during the hot summers of their youth and wished he could go back to those innocent times.

Accusing Olivia of lying had been unfair. She wouldn't do that. If he'd learned anything about her, it was that she had a great deal of integrity.

What woman, when faced with the prospect of never becoming a mother, wouldn't deny the possibility? Especially someone who adored children the way Olivia did. He'd watched her with the twins. He'd seen how his daughters had bonded with Olivia. She'd won them over with her generous, kind heart. They'd been as helpless against her sweetness as he'd been.

By now his parents would be discussing damage control. And debating how to proceed. Olivia had understood the position this news report had put him in. They would advise him against marrying a woman whose fertility was in question. But he wouldn't make any decisions until he knew the extent of her problems.

And if she could never have children?

He would need to address the bargain he'd struck with her father. The deal with Lord Darcy was contingent on Olivia becoming Gabriel's wife.

Talk about being stuck between a rock and a hard place. No matter what decision he made, he would fail Sherdana.

Two hours later he entered the salon in the family section of the south wing and found everyone assembled.

His sister came forward to give him a hug. "Did you check on Olivia?"

"I went for a ride."

His father regarded him with a frown, his opinion clear. Gabriel ignored him and went to sit beside his mother. He'd come to a preliminary decision and knew it wouldn't meet with everyone's approval.

"I needed some time to think."

The king fixed Gabriel with a hard stare. "How do you intend to handle this?"

"Handle?" Gabriel hadn't considered how they should approach the press about this latest bombshell. "We could start by sending out a press release downplaying the serious nature of Olivia's problems, but I'm not sure with her doctor's records as proof, this is going to do us much good."

"I meant with Olivia," the king said, his voice a low rumble.

Gabriel became aware that his entire family was watching him and waiting for his answer. It was as if the occupants of the room had stopped breathing.

"What do you mean?" Gabriel asked, certain he knew where his father was going with the question, but needing to hear it asked out loud.

"You need a wife who can bear children."

In other words, he must break his engagement with Olivia and reexamine the dozen or so women he'd rejected when he chose her.

"And what am I to say to Lord Darcy? That his daughter's only value to me lies in her ability to produce heirs?" His father's glower told Gabriel he'd stepped into dangerous territory with his sarcasm. At the moment, Gabriel didn't care. What could his father do? For a moment, Gabriel reveled in rebellion. As a teenager, he'd been the best behaved of his siblings, getting into trouble rarely and then never with anything serious.

Nic had started a fire in his room at fifteen experimenting with rockets. Christian had "borrowed" their uncle's Ferrari when he was fourteen and gone joyriding. The expensive sports car had ended up half submerged in a ditch and Christian had been disciplined, but that had only temporarily slowed him down, not stopped him completely.

Gabriel had shouldered his future responsibility like a dutiful son and the newspapers had been filled with photos of him accompanying his mother on her visits to the hospital and various other charitable events and headlines about how lucky Sherdana was to have such a shining example of youth for their next monarch.

"I had fertility problems, as well," the queen reminded her husband, breaking the tension between father and son.

"But neither of us had any idea before we married," the king said, sending his wife a stern look.

"Yet despite your need for an heir, you didn't set me aside when my troubles came to light."

"We'd been married two years. How could I have let you go?"

Gabriel saw the unspoken communication that passed between his parents and felt a flare of envy. The emotion didn't surprise him. He'd felt twinges of it before when watching his parents in private. They were so in sync with each other. He'd hoped for just a little of that depth of intimacy in his own marriage and had begun to believe he'd find it with Olivia.

"Olivia and I will talk later this afternoon."

"You are intending to break off the engagement."

"I'm not sure that's necessary." He saw his father's brows come together. "She claims she had surgery to correct the problem. We need to discuss the situation in more depth and consult a doctor before I make such a radical decision."

The door flew open without a warning knock, catching everyone's attention. Stewart stood in the open doorway, his face stark with concern.

"Forgive my interruption," he said, bowing in apology. "Something has happened to Lady Darcy."

Gabriel's heart jumped in his chest. He surged to his feet and crossed the room in three strides. "What's wrong?"

"I don't know. Miss Marshall said she's locked herself in the bathroom and won't answer the door."

"What makes you think something has happened to her?"

"Her clothes are all over the suite and they've been shredded."

Cursing, Gabriel lunged past his secretary and raced down the hallway. Stewart's long legs usually made him a match for Gabriel, but he had to resort to jogging to keep up.

When Gabriel entered the suite, he registered the destruction in passing but didn't stop. He rushed over to join Olivia's private secretary, who was at the bathroom door, knocking and calling for her to answer. Shoving her aside, Gabriel kicked in the door.

When the door frame gave and the door shot open, the metallic tang of blood immediately hit him. Olivia lay on the cold tile, a large crimson patch on her pale blue skirt. Panic tore through him.

"Call an ambulance!" He dropped to his knees beside her and was relieved to see her chest rise and fall. "When did you enter the suite?" he demanded of her private secretary.

"Perhaps ten minutes ago. I called to her but she didn't open the door or answer. And from what had happened to her clothes I knew something had to be wrong."

How long had she been bleeding like this? Gabriel clenched his teeth and fought the fear rising inside him. She couldn't die. He wouldn't let that happen.

"Get me a blanket off the bed. We're going to take her to the hospital."

Libby did as she was told. "What about the ambulance?"

"There isn't time." Besides, he didn't think he could sit around and watch Olivia slowly bleed to death without going crazy. He'd always prided himself on thought before action, but right now, he was thinking of nothing but saving the woman he'd been yelling at no more than three hours earlier.

Forget that. Focus on getting Olivia to the hospital.

He wrapped her lower half in the blanket and scooped her into his arms. His family had arrived in the hallway just outside the suite. He brushed past his father and brother without answering their offers of help. Olivia was his fiancée. His responsibility.

And he blamed himself for her current crisis. Somehow he knew that if he'd been more approachable, if so much pressure hadn't been brought to bear on her, Olivia might have talked to him about her fertility problems and a safe solution might have been reached.

The limo was waiting at the bottom of the stairs. He settled her into the backseat and cradled her body in his lap. Only then did he become aware of the thundering of his heart. The painful pounding in his chest wasn't caused by carrying her through the palace, but by the sight of her utter stillness and pallor. As the car raced through the palace gates, it finally hit home just how bad this situation was.

"Faster," he growled to the driver as he hooked his finger around a strand of her blond hair and pulled it away from her lips.

The car's powerful engine roared as they sped through the city, but the fifteen-minute drive had never felt so long.

Gabriel brushed his lips across Olivia's forehead and silently pleaded with her to hang on and fight. *Like you fought for her?* Gabriel tried to tune out the mocking inner voice, but guilt sliced at him.

At the hospital's emergency entrance, five people in scrubs crowded the car as soon as it stopped. Stewart must have called ahead and warned them he was coming. They got Olivia situated on a stretcher and took her away before he had a chance to say a word. He rushed toward the glass doors in their wake, catching bits of medical jargon as they sped the unconscious woman inside.

He'd expected to be allowed into the treatment room with her, but a nurse blocked his way.

"Let the doctors work," she said, her voice kind but firm.

He might have ten inches and eighty pounds on her, but Gabriel sensed that the nurse could stop him if he tried to go past.

"How soon will I know something?"

"I'll make sure someone keeps you informed."

"She's lost a lot of blood," he said.

"We know."

She herded him into a private waiting room and offered coffee. Gabriel stared at her, unable to comprehend why this woman was behaving in such a mundane manner while Olivia was down the hall struggling for her life.

"No," he snapped, and then moderated his tone. "Thank you. All I need is information."

She nodded and headed off.

Left alone, Gabriel dropped his head into his hands and surrendered to despair. She couldn't die. She couldn't leave him. He wasn't sure how to step into the future, to become king without her by his side. They would figure a way around her infertility. He recalled his mother's words. She, too, had struggled to produce the heir her husband so desperately needed. When natural methods had failed, she'd gotten help from specialists. And now, she had four children to show for it.

He and Olivia would find specialists, as well. They would have children together.

"Gabriel?"

A hand touched his shoulder. He lifted his head and stared up into his sister's face. She touched his cheek and her fingertips came away with a trace of moisture.

"Is she?" Ariana gasped, seeing his expression.

He shook his head, guessing what conclusion she'd leaped to. "They're working on her now."

"Any word how she's doing?"

"No. The nurse said they'd keep me informed, but she hasn't been back." He glanced at his watch. "That was thirty minutes ago."

What had been happening while he'd been lost in thought? Anxiety flared that he'd had no news. How bad had things gone since she'd been taken away from him?

"She's going to be all right, Gabriel," Ariana said, moving toward him.

Standing, Gabriel wrapped his arms around his sister. She pushed her body against his to offer comfort.

"Your Majesties. Prince Gabriel. Princess Ariana." A

solemn man of average height in pale green scrubs stood five feet away from the royal pair. "I'm Dr. Warner."

Gabriel felt Ariana's tight embrace squeeze his ribs even harder and appreciated her support. "How's Olivia?"

"I won't sugarcoat it. Not good. She's lost a lot of blood." The doctor looked even grimmer as he delivered the next bit of news. "She's still hemorrhaging. We've sent her up to the OR."

A primal cry of denial gathered in Gabriel's chest. "What aren't you telling us?" he demanded.

"The only way to save her may be a hysterectomy. Naturally we will do everything possible to avoid such a drastic procedure."

"Do whatever it takes to save her life." Gabriel pinned the doctor with his gaze, making sure the man understood. "Whatever it takes."

Ten

The first time Olivia opened her eyes, she was aware of nothing but pain. It stabbed at her like slivers of broken glass. Then, something changed. The hurt eased and she fell backward into darkness.

The next time she surfaced, she kept herself awake longer. But not by much. Voices reached her ears, but the speakers were too far away for her to catch individual words. And the pain was back. All she wanted to do was escape into numbness.

They said the third time's the charm. Olivia wasn't sure she agreed when next she regained consciousness. Her body ached. No. Not her body, her abdomen.

Breathless with fear, she stared around the hospital room. It was empty. She was alone.

She felt hollow. Like a balloon filled with air.

The last thing she recalled was fighting with Gabriel. Where was he? Did he know she was in the hospital? Did he even care? Her heart contracted.

"Good to see you awake," a nurse said as she entered the room. "How's your pain?"

"Manageable." Her mouth felt stuffed with cotton. "May I have some water?"

The nurse brought a cup close and placed the straw between Olivia's lips. She sipped gratefully, then sagged back against the pillow, exhausted by the simple movement.

"I feel so weak."

"You've been through a lot."

"What happened to me?"

"The doctor will be along in a little while to talk to you."

Without energy to argue, Olivia closed her eyes and let her mind drift. The silence pressed on her, heightening her tension. She fought to clear her head, sought her last memory. Her period had been heavier than ever before. And the cramping... She'd been afraid, depressed. Gingerly she sent her fingertips questing for the source of her discomfort. Pain shot through her as she pressed on her lower abdomen.

Just then, the door opened again and a handsome older man in scrubs came in. "Good afternoon. I'm Dr. Warner."

"I wish I could say it's nice to meet you."

"I understand. You've been through a tough time."

"What happened to me?" Her mind sharpened as anxiety filled her.

"You were hemorrhaging, and we had a difficult time stopping your blood loss." He plucked her chart out of a pocket attached to the foot of the bed and scrutinized it. "How's your pain?"

"About a six." She waited while he jotted something down on her chart before asking, "How did you stop the hemorrhaging?"

"Surgery." He met her gaze. "It was an extensive procedure."

He hadn't said anything specific, but his expression told her just how extensive the surgery had been.

"I'm never going to have children, am I?"

"I'm sorry. The only way we could stop the bleeding was to remove your uterus."

Olivia shut her eyes to escape the sympathy in the man's face. Denial exploded in her head. She clutched the bed rails, desperate for something to ground her as the world tipped sideways. A wail began in her chest. She clenched her teeth to contain it as a lifetime of discipline and order asserted itself. She would grieve later. In private.

"I know that this will be a difficult adjustment. You are very young to have undergone such a drastic change."

"Who knows?" she whispered.

He looked taken aback. "Your father. The royal family."

"The media?"

"Of course not." Dr. Warner looked appalled.

"Is my father here?"

"He's in the waiting room with Prince Gabriel. I spoke with him an hour ago."

"Could I see him, please? No one else, just my father."

"I'll have the nurse fetch him for you."

But the man who showed up next wasn't a sixty-year-old British earl with gray hair and a neat beard, but a tall, hollow-eyed man with a dark shadow blurring his knife-sharp jawline. Olivia's heartbeat accelerated as Gabriel advanced into the room, his clothes rumpled, his face a mask. He reached out to cover her hand with his, but she moved it away just in time.

"I'm sorry," she said, unable to lift her gaze higher than the open collar of his white shirt. "I should have told you about my medical issues. I just thought that everything was going to be okay."

"You gave us a scare." He pulled a chair beside her bed and lowered himself into it. This put him at eye level with her and made avoiding his fierce golden gaze that much harder. "When I found you on the floor of the bathroom unconscious." His tone made it hard for Olivia to breathe. "I thought…" He shook his head.

"I'm sorry. I had no idea that quitting the pill was going to cause this much…" To her dismay a sob popped out. Just like that. No warning. No chance to swallow it or choke on it. Then tears were streaming down her face and Gabriel was stroking her hair and squeezing her hand. His gentleness only made her feel worse.

"Olivia, I'm so sorry."

He placed her palm against his cheek. The warmth beneath her fingers spread up her arm and drifted through her entire body as she took in the aching sadness in his eyes.

"I'm going to be fine," she lied, hating how much she wanted to lean on him for support. Choking on her misery, she barreled on. "At least now there's no question whether I can have children. You'll never have to wonder if by marrying me you made a huge mistake."

"Marrying you would never have been a mistake."

But if she'd had difficulty getting pregnant, he couldn't help but blame her.

"That's a moot point." She willed herself to be strong and to make the break quick and final. "We can't marry now."

"I'm not giving up on us." He covered her hand with his and regarded her with somber eyes.

"There is no more us, Gabriel." She tugged her hand free. "You are going to be king of Sherdana one day. You need to put your country's needs first."

"I have two brothers—"

"Please." She couldn't bear to hear any more. Anything he said would encourage her to be optimistic and the last thing she needed to do was hope everything was going to be okay. "I'm really tired. And I'm in pain. I just want to see my father."

He looked as if he wanted to argue with her. She shook her head and closed her eyes. Another tear trickled down her cheek, but she ignored it.

"And I think it would be better if you don't visit me again."

"I can't accept that."

"Please, Gabriel."

He exhaled harshly. "I'll get your father."

She waited to open her eyes until his soft footfalls receded. Her fingers tingled from contact with Gabriel's cheek. It brought to mind all those times when her hands had roamed over him, exploring his masculine contours, learning all the delightful ways his body differed from hers.

Reaching toward a nearby box of tissues exhausted her. The weakness was frustrating. Before she had the chance to lose herself in the black cloud of misery that hovered nearby, her father entered the room. His embrace stirred up her emotions again and Olivia began to cry once more. This time, however, she didn't feel the need to hold back. His shirt was soaked by the time she ran out of tears.

"I want to go home," she told him, making use of the tissue box once again.

"The doctor wants to keep you in here for at least a week."

"Can't I be transferred to a hospital in London?"

"You are in no shape to travel." He patted her hand. "It's just a week. Then I'll take you home."

A week. It was too long. More than her body needed to heal and that wouldn't be possible until she was miles and miles from Sherdana and its prince.

Shortly after speaking with Olivia, Gabriel returned to the palace alone, his emotions in turmoil. Staff scattered as he crossed the expansive foyer, heading for his office. The way they disappeared he must have looked like the devil himself had come calling.

It had shocked him that after she'd survived her brush with death, her first act would be to end their engagement. She'd done it gracefully, shouldering the responsibility, leaving him free to move on with a clear conscience.

"Move on."

He spat out the words like the foulest curse. No matter how angry he'd been when he found out about her medical condition, he'd not really considered ending things. How could he ever replace Olivia in his life after making love with her? Watching her with his daughters? Seeing that damned tattoo. *Hope.* He could sure use some right now.

Entering his office, he flung himself into a chair near the cold fireplace. He'd been up all night. Exhaustion should be eating into his bones and muscles, but rage burned white-hot in his veins. He massaged his temples where a headache had begun the minute he'd walked out of Olivia's hospital room. Or perhaps it had been there all along. Up until that moment, he'd been completely focused on Olivia.

But after leaving her bedside, he realized that his role in her life was over. As was her role in his. From now on they would be nothing more than familiar strangers. He would probably not exchange a dozen words with her before she left for England and her old life.

God, his chest ached.

"Your Highness?" Gabriel's secretary had poked his head in the door.

"Not now, Stewart."

He needed some time to adjust. How much time, he didn't know. He'd never imagined having to live without Olivia and he wasn't going to pretend that he could just shake off this tragedy and continue on.

"Your Highness," Stewart persisted. "Your father, the king, wants to speak with you."

"I know my father is the king," Gabriel said, taking his annoyance out on his private secretary. He pushed out of the chair, deciding to face whatever his father had to say now rather that make the king wait until he'd showered and changed.

He found his father on the phone in his office and went

to pour himself a shot of scotch while he waited for him to conclude the call.

"A little early for that, isn't it?" the king demanded as he hung up.

"I think a man's entitled to a drink after his fiancée breaks up with him, don't you?"

The king shot him a hard glance as he rose to his feet and crossed to the tray with the coffeepot and cups. Pouring a cup, he plucked the crystal tumbler from Gabriel's finger and replaced it with bone china.

"I just got off the phone with Lord Darcy. He told me you and Olivia ended things."

Ah, so the old man was pulling his offer to set up a company since his daughter was no longer going to be Sherdana's queen. Gabriel shrugged. He didn't really blame the earl for changing his mind.

"She ended it," he said. "But don't worry. Christian will find us some other prospective investors." He sipped the coffee and regarded his father over the brim. "Perhaps one of them will even have an eligible daughter since apparently I'm back on the market."

The king let Gabriel's bitter comment pass unanswered. "Naturally, I would like to continue pursuing other companies, but the need isn't urgent. Darcy is going forward with his plans."

Gabriel's cup hit the saucer with a clatter. From his contact with Lord Darcy, he knew the man was a hardheaded businessman. Sherdana was a good choice for expansion, but not his only and not necessarily his best.

Olivia.

This was her doing.

The exhaustion he'd expected to feel earlier washed over him now. Gabriel wavered on his feet. "Olivia must have told him to honor the commitment. There's no other reason for Darcy to proceed."

"But if she knows you're not getting married, why would she persuade her father to honor his commitment to us?"

"Because that's the sort of woman she is," Gabriel said. "Honorable. The sort who doesn't go back on a promise. Unlike me," he finished in an undertone.

This time, his bitterness was too much for his father to ignore. "You are not reneging on a promise to Lady Darcy," the king said. "She understands she will never be able to give you an heir and has graciously ended your engagement."

That's when it hit him. He didn't want their engagement to end.

Olivia had promised to marry him. And if she was as honorable as he'd just described, she still would.

After six endless days in the hospital, with pain and grief her constant companions, Olivia was an empty shell in both body and soul. For the majority of her stay she'd lain with her eyes closed, floating on a tide of pain medication that dulled the ache in her lower abdomen but couldn't blunt the agony in her heart. With her ability to bear children ripped from her, she shrank from her future. Abandoned by optimism, tears filled her eyes and ran unheeded down her cheeks. Her losses were too much to bear.

On the third day of her incarceration, Libby had smuggled in her favorite chocolate. Olivia had put on a show of courage for her private secretary, but left alone once more, she'd retreated to the dark place where she contemplated what her life had become.

Then, this morning, twenty-four hours before she was scheduled for release, she instructed Libby to bring her files so she could compile a list of all the things she'd committed to in the past month.

"Are you sure you should be taxing yourself with this?" Libby protested, a dozen files clutched to her chest.

Olivia indicated that she wanted the files placed on the rolling tray positioned over her bed. "I've got to find something to keep my mind busy, or I'll go completely mad."

Libby did as she was told and then retreated to the guest chair with her laptop. "Prince Gabriel…" the private secretary began, breaking off when Olivia shook her head.

"How are Bethany and Karina?"

"They miss you." Libby opened the laptop and stared at the screen. "Everyone at the palace misses you."

Not wishing to go down that path, Olivia changed the subject. "Have they found Marissa's sister yet?"

"I'm afraid not."

The memory of the woman's attack had resurfaced a couple days after Olivia had woken up. It hadn't struck her as odd that no one asked about the incident because she'd assumed Marissa's sister had fled the palace with no one being the wiser.

When she'd shared the story with Libby, Olivia had learned what had happened after she'd passed out in the bathroom. She'd given herself a couple seconds to regret the loss of her wardrobe and then insisted on telling her story to palace security and the police.

"Her apartment in Milan is being watched," Libby continued, "but she hasn't returned there. From what I gather, she hasn't contacted her friends in six months. But I'm sure Prince Gabriel will not be satisfied until she's caught."

"I'll feel better when that happens," Olivia said, and opened the file sitting on top of the pile. It was a budget proposal for some improvements to a school she sponsored in Kenya.

The mundane work soothed her spirit. Nothing better for the soul than to worry about someone else's problems.

Ariana and Christian visited several times in the next

few days and brought regards from the king and queen as well as flowers. But Gabriel had been absent. She'd sent him away and asked Libby to make certain he understood that she wanted him to maintain his distance. Her grief was still too strong. She wasn't ready to face him. Not until she came to terms with the end of her engagement and her empty future.

"Prince Gabriel is desperately worried about you," Libby said.

As sweet as it was for Libby to say, Olivia doubted her use of the word *desperately*.

"I hope you've told him I'm recovering nicely."

"He might like to see that for himself."

Olivia's throat tightened and she shook her head. The words blurred on the sheet of paper she held in her hand and she blinked to clear her vision.

"He really cares for you. It's obvious." Libby sat forward, her eyes bright and intense. "I don't think I've ever seen a man so distraught as when we thought you might die. He commanded the doctor to do whatever it took to save you."

Joy dispelled Olivia's gloom for a moment as she let herself warm to Libby's interpretation of events. "Of course he cares," she agreed, wishing the situation was as simple as that. "We became…close these last few weeks. But he needs an heir. That's something I can't give him."

"But you love him. Surely that counts for more." Libby spoke quietly as if afraid of how Olivia would react to her audacity.

Olivia starting drawing circles on the notepad. She did love Gabriel, but he must never know. She didn't want to burden him with something like that. He already had enough guilt on his shoulders with Marissa. He didn't need to suffer even more regret because another woman entertained a desperate and impossible love for him.

"I love him, but please do not tell a soul," she rushed on as Libby's face lit up. "Prince Gabriel needs to find someone new to marry. I don't want him thinking of me at all as he goes about courting his future bride."

The thought of Gabriel with another woman made her heart ache, but she fought the pain.

Libby's delight became determination. "I really think he needs to know."

Olivia offered her friend a sad smile. "He can't. Sherdana deserves a queen who can have children."

"What about what you deserve?" Libby pushed. "Don't you deserve to be happy?"

"I will be," she assured her secretary. "My life isn't over. I'm just starting a new chapter. Not the one I expected to be starting, but how often do we get exactly what we expect?"

Eleven

Staring at pictures of women he'd rejected six months ago wasn't stimulating Gabriel's appetite for lunch.

"What do you think of Reinette du Piney?" his mother asked, sliding an eight-by-ten head shot of a very beautiful brunette across the table toward him.

"She's pigeon-toed," he replied, slipping his spoon beneath a carrot and lifting it free of the broth. "What exactly is it I'm eating?"

"Creamy carrot soup with anise. The chef is experimenting again."

"You really must stop him from inflicting his culinary curiosity on us."

"Gabriel, you cannot reject du Piney because she's pigeon-toed."

He wasn't. He was rejecting her because the only woman he wanted to marry had made it clear she was going to do the right thing for Sherdana even if he wouldn't.

In the meantime, his mother had persisted in starting the search for his future wife all over again, despite Gabriel's refusal to contribute anything positive.

"I'm only thinking of our children," he countered, setting his spoon down and tossing his napkin over it. "Imagine how they'd be teased at school if they inherited their mother's unfortunate trait."

"Your children will not be teased at school because

they will be tutored at home the way you and your siblings were." His mother sifted through the pictures and pulled out another. "What about Amelia? You liked her."

"She was pleasant enough. But I think her husband would take umbrage with me for poaching his wife."

"Bother."

Gabriel might have felt like smiling at his mother's equivalent of a curse if he wasn't feeling so damned surly. Olivia had left the hospital a few days ago and was staying at the Royal Caron Hotel until her surgeon cleared her for travel. By bribing the man with an enormous donation toward updating the hospital with digital radiology, Gabriel had succeeded in keeping her in Sherdana longer than necessary. He'd hoped she would let him apologize to her in person, but she adamantly refused to see him.

"Gabriel, are you listening to me?"

"I'm not going to marry any of these women."

His mother sat back and stared at him, her eyes narrowed and searching. "Have you decided on someone else?"

"Yes. The same person I've wanted all along."

"Olivia."

"You don't sound surprised."

"You take after your father. He's a romantic devil, too." Her eyes sparkled at Gabriel's doubtful expression. "Oh, not that anyone other than me would know it, but he wouldn't consider divorcing me when I couldn't get pregnant. Even after I left him and made him think that I'd fallen in love with another man."

"What?" This was a tale he'd never heard. "You fell in love with someone while you were married to Father?"

His mother laughed gaily. "Of course not. But I certainly convinced your father I did." A faraway look entered her eyes. "But he chased after me and discovered there was no other man. I finally admitted that the doctor told me I couldn't get pregnant the old-fashioned way and together we figured out a solution."

That sounded familiar. Except for the part where a solution was found together.

"I'm surprised," Gabriel admitted.

"Because your father counseled you to break your engagement with Olivia even before the hysterectomy? You need to understand how difficult those days were for us. The doubt, the worry. It was hard on us. Hard on our marriage. And we were deeply in love."

Her last words struck a nerve. "And Olivia and I are not." His mother's assumption annoyed him more than it should.

Given that he'd only just begun to get acquainted with the woman he had been planning to marry, it made sense that he couldn't possibly love her.

And if not love, then what emotion was at the root of his miserable existence without Olivia?

"He just wants to spare you." She reached across the table and laid her hand over his. "We both do."

Gabriel captured her gaze. "Would you change anything about the decision you made? Knowing the trials and heartbreak you suffered, would you walk away from the man you love and never look back?"

His mother withdrew her hand and sat back. Her expression was determined and sad at the same time. "No."

"Thank you."

He stood and circled the table to kiss her cheek. Expecting her to ask what he was up to, she surprised him again by staying silent.

Leaving his mother, he headed upstairs to await Olivia's arrival. She'd made arrangements through his mother to visit Bethany and Karina and bring them a special birthday present. Gabriel knew it was cheating to use his daughters to secure time with Olivia, but he was feeling a little desperate. If his daughters had taught him anything it was how to exist in the moment. There was no past or future with them. They lived for hugs, treats, mischief and pony rides. Every second in their company reminded him that wonderful things came out of less than ideal situations.

The twins weren't in the nursery. He'd arranged for them to have a picnic in the garden. In half an hour they would arrive for their nap. He hoped that gave him enough time with Olivia. While he waited, he sat on Bethany's bed and picked up the photo of Marissa on the girls' nightstand. A scrapbook had been among the twins' possessions. Olivia had chosen this particular picture to frame and place between the girls so they would remember their mother.

Marissa was pregnant in the picture. Not full-term, perhaps seven months, yet still huge. Had she known she was carrying twins? He traced her smile with his fingertips. She looked older than he remembered, aged by experience, not years, yet luminescent in motherhood.

Why hadn't she contacted him when she knew she was pregnant? Had she not wished to burden him? Had she feared his rejection yet again? He couldn't have married her. Wouldn't have married her. Even if Sherdana's laws hadn't dictated his bride needed to be a citizen of the country or of noble birth for his offspring to be able to inherit the crown, where Gabriel and Marissa had been most compatible was between the sheets, which was where they'd spent half of their time together.

Out of bed, her passionate nature had revealed itself in turbulent emotions and insecurity. He knew the latter had been his fault. He couldn't offer her a future and she'd deserved better. In the end, he'd let her go and part of him had been relieved.

He'd put Sherdana's needs before hers. He'd done the same with Olivia. Only this time there was no certainty that he'd made the right decision. No sense that a burden had been lifted from his shoulders. His daughters were the only bright spot in his future. His mother wanted him to consider who would become his princess, but he couldn't make that decision until he spoke with Olivia and saw for himself what was in her heart.

Olivia took on the challenge of the palace stairs at a sedate pace, but was uncomfortably short of breath by the time she reached the first landing. Several maids trotted past her, but none of the staff paid her undue attention. Still, she felt like an interloper in the place where she thought she'd spend the rest of her life.

Relaxing her grip on the gaily wrapped packages containing china dolls, Olivia forced herself to keep climbing. As beautiful as the dolls were, giving toddlers such delicate toys was probably a recipe for disaster. But Olivia wanted to share with the girls something special. The dolls were just like the one her mother had bought for her and not lived to present the gift.

In her heart Olivia knew it was selfish of her to want them to remember her. First their mother had died and now they faced the loss of someone else they relied on. It was too much change for ones so young. At least they would still have their father. Olivia was comforted by how much Gabriel loved his daughters.

In two days the twins turned two. The party Olivia had spent weeks planning had stirred the palace into new heights of frantic activity. As much as Olivia wanted to go, attending was out of the question. Even though she knew the twins would want her there, they were undoubtedly the only members of the royal family who would.

Who could blame them? Olivia knew the end of her engagement to Gabriel had driven the media into a frenzy of speculation about whom he might choose for his next bride. Social networks had blown up with news about the top two candidates. As long as Olivia remained in the picture, the news outlets would stir the pot. It was better if she disappeared from Sherdana. But she couldn't go without saying goodbye to Bethany and Karina.

Her slow rise to the second floor gave Olivia lots of time to remember how golden her future had seemed the first time she'd ascended these stairs and to brood about the handsome prince who'd never be hers.

Coming to the palace was a risk. She might run into Gabriel and lose the modicum of peace she'd made with her situation. At the same time, she was foolishly excited at the thought of running into Gabriel again. Even knowing they could never be together didn't stop her from longing to see him one last time.

It was irrational, but she'd been hurt that he'd heeded her desire for no further contact after her surgery. She'd broken things off. While part of her was relieved that he'd honored her wishes, her less rational side had resented Gabriel for taking her at her word.

But what truly upset her was, after everything that had happened, she continued to crave his company. She woke from dreams where he held her close and whispered she was his life, his dearest love, and discovered she was alone. And all along, her heart hung heavy in her chest. Emptiness lingered below the stinging incision in her abdomen. Depression coiled about her thoughts, threatening to smother her. A dozen get-well bouquets brightened her hotel suite but couldn't pierce the fog surrounding her emotions.

Olivia paused at the top step and leaned on the banister to catch her breath before proceeding down the hall to the nursery. She knew the twins would be finishing up lunch and had chosen this time to visit because it limited how long she would stay.

When she got to the nursery, she stopped just inside the

doorway, but didn't see the twins. Instead, Gabriel occupied the space. Her heart gave a giddy leap. He sat on Bethany's bed, a silver frame in his hands, fingertips tenderly resting on the face of the woman in the photo. Marissa.

His expression held such sorrow, his mouth drooping in regret as she'd never seen before. Her heart wept for his obvious grief, but the tears that sprang to her eyes weren't for Gabriel; they were for herself. She'd believed him when he claimed to be over Marissa, but three years later he continued to grieve for what could never be. Was that how she looked in those unguarded moments when she thought about all she'd lost? Was this what it looked like when a heart shattered?

Suddenly this errand didn't seem like a good idea. She should have let Libby bring Bethany and Karina to the hotel instead of returning to the palace. But the media had camped out in front of the hotel in the hope that she'd comment on her broken engagement. During the short walk from lobby door to car, Olivia had worn dark glasses and a wide brimmed hat to prevent the photographers from catching a newsworthy photo of her. Olivia couldn't put the girls in the middle of the chaos.

"Olivia!"

Gabriel's head snapped up at the enthusiastic cries coming from behind her. His gaze crashed into hers. She wobbled beneath the triple impact of the twins wrapping their arms around her hips and the raw emotion in Gabriel's eyes.

The twins' demands for attention offered her no chance to react to what she'd seen, but she was glad. Remaining upright as they pressed against her became that much harder thanks to the bulky, delicate bundles she carried.

Gabriel stepped forward and took the packages from her. "Girls, be gentle with Olivia. She's been sick and is very fragile."

The glow in his eyes warmed her head to toe as he extricated her from the twins' enthusiastic embrace. She had a hard time looking away.

"Don't like sick," Bethany proclaimed, her lower lip slipping forward.

Karina gave her head a vigorous shake.

"I'm much better now, but still a little sore. Like when you skin your knee how it takes a while to stop hurting."

Karina bent down to touch Olivia's unblemished knees. "Hurt?"

Olivia laughed. "No, angel. My knees are okay. My hurt is here." She pointed to her stomach.

"Can we see?" Bethany demanded.

Olivia gestured toward the packages Gabriel had set on their beds. "Why don't you open your birthday presents instead."

"Birthday."

Olivia smiled past her sadness at having to go home to England and never see these girls again. "They are very special. I hope you like them."

While the girls tore into the wrapping, Olivia watched them, but her attention was captured by the tall man who stood so close beside her. It seemed the worst sort of torture not to lean into his strength and forget about the past week. But the twinges in her abdomen kept her grounded in reality.

"That was a lovely gift," Gabriel said as the girls fell to exclaiming over the dolls' hair and wardrobe.

"Something for them to remember me by." Emotion seized her by the throat. "I didn't realize leaving them was going to be so hard."

"You could stay longer."

Olivia flinched at how her heart leaped with hope. "I can't, and it's not fair of you to ask."

Why would he even want her to stay? He knew as well

as she did that having her around would create problems for him both in the media and in his search for a bride.

"A lot of things haven't been fair lately." He brushed her hair off one shoulder, grazing her skin in the process.

To Olivia's immense shock, desire sparked. How was it possible after all she'd been through? She looked up to see if Gabriel had noticed her reaction and to her dismay, he had.

"Olivia." His deep voice rumbled in his chest, creating a matching vibration in her. "We need to talk." He found her hand with his.

The slide of his fingers against hers made her heart race. "I think we've said everything there is to say."

"Maybe you have, but I have a few things you need to hear."

Olivia's gaze shot toward the twins. To her relief, they were oblivious to the charged undercurrents passing between her and Gabriel. The girls had been through enough and didn't deserve to witness them arguing. She turned her back to them and pitched her voice to carry no farther than the foot that separated her from Gabriel.

"Don't do this. There's nothing you have to say that I want to hear. What I need is to leave this country and forget all about you."

"Can you do that?" he murmured, his free hand cupping the side of her face, his tender touch bringing tears to her eyes. "Can you forget me? Forget how it was between us?"

Harsh emotions sandblasted her nerves raw. "Would you want me to do otherwise?"

"Yes. Stay and fight—"

"Fight?" The word gusted out of her on a bitter laugh. "I have nothing left to fight with. It's gone, Gabriel. My ability to bear children. My chance to be a mother. I'm nothing more than a shell." An empty shell without him. "I just want to go home and forget."

Forget how his smile transformed her.

Forget how it felt to fall asleep in his arms.

Forget how much she loved him.

"Can you?" He cupped the back of her neck and pulled her gently against his powerful, muscular body. "Can you forget me?"

Her pulse danced with erotic longing. She tore her gaze away from the sensual light in his eyes that drew her like a candle in the darkness. How was it possible she could want him with such intensity when the parts that made her a whole woman were gone?

He lowered his voice to a husky murmur. "Because I will never be able to forget you."

It wasn't fair of him to tell her that. To tantalize her with longing for what could never be.

Contact with him seared her from breast to thigh. Her incision burned the way it had during those first few days, reminding her that she'd have a permanent mark on her body that would never let her forget.

"Maybe not forget," she told him, keeping her voice soft to hide its unsteadiness. "But you'll move on and be happy."

Before he could respond, they were struck from two sides by the twins. Sandwiched between them, Olivia had no way to escape Gabriel. He saw her predicament and a predatory smile curved his lips before they descended to hers.

Sweet sunshine washed through her body as she surrendered to the delicious drag of his mouth against hers. This was where she belonged. To this man. And these girls. The family she craved.

Her whole world contracted to Gabriel's kiss and the twins' hugs. A great rushing sound filled her ears, drowning out her inner voice and all the reasons why this couldn't be her future. Loving Gabriel had never seemed so easy.

Outside pressure didn't exist. She was free to express herself, to tell him what was truly in her heart.

I love you.

But she never uttered the words because the girls clamored for their own share of Olivia's attention as the kiss fell apart. Her lips tingled in the aftermath as Gabriel held her close a moment longer before letting her step back.

"Tea party. Tea party," Bethany called.

Karina seized her and pulled.

It took her a couple seconds to realize that the girls were referring to the small table set up near the window. She shook her head. "It's your nap time."

"Girls, Olivia is right. Hattie will read to you after you lie down."

While it hurt to kneel and give hugs and kisses to each of the toddlers, Olivia braved the pain for one last goodbye. By the time they had been persuaded to let her go, Olivia's sorrow had rendered her mute.

Gabriel seemed to understand her distress because he waited until they'd descended to the grand hall before speaking. "When are you leaving?"

"My final doctor's appointment is later this week. I expect to be able to travel after that."

"You really should come to the twins' birthday party. You planned everything. It's only right that you be there."

Temptation trembled through her. It would be so easy to agree, to prolong the final parting for another day. But what good would that do? She'd have one more memory to keep her awake at night.

"I think it's better that we said our goodbyes now."

"I don't agree." He took her hand and stopped her from leaving. His gold eyes were somber as he met her gaze. "Bethany and Karina will be sad if you don't come."

His touch made her want to turn back the clock. If she'd not been so rash as to stop taking the pill against her doctor's order, she would be marrying Gabriel in a week. Then again, the burden of producing an heir to the kingdom would still be weighing heavily on her.

"And I'm not ready to say goodbye," he said, interrupting her thoughts.

She delighted at his words, until she recalled how he'd looked at that photo of Marissa. Three years ago he'd turned his back on her and chosen his country instead. Olivia had seen the way he'd been tortured by that choice every time he looked at his daughters. Was he hoping that putting his country's needs second this time would somehow redeem him for failing Marissa?

She eased her hand free. "You already have. The second the story of my fertility issues made it to prime time any chance of us getting married was gone." She touched his arm in sympathy. "People in our positions don't belong to themselves."

"That's true," he murmured, seizing her chin and forcing her to look at him. "You belong to me."

She jerked away and took a step back. "I don't." But her blood sang another tune. She was his, heart and soul. There would be no other.

"Deny it all you want, but I was the first man who made love to you. The first man you loved. That sort of bond may stretch but it will not break."

Her pulse rocked at his use of the word *love*. Did he know the depth of her feelings for him? She'd not been particularly careful to guard her emotions during those long hours in his arms. Had he figured out the truth or was he simply referring to the physical act of loving?

"Why are you saying these things? Do you think leaving is easy for me?" She spied the front door and knew her reprieve was mere steps away, but she had a few hard truths to deliver first. "I was planning on making my life here with you. It hurts more than I can say that I can't marry you. Asking me to stay is completely—"

"Selfish," he interrupted, lifting her palm to his lips. "You're right. I am selfish."

When he released her hand, Olivia clenched her fingers around the kiss. His blunt admission had dimmed her frustration. This impossible situation was of her making. If only she'd told him of her fertility issues. He never would have proposed. She never would have fallen in love with him.

"You have a right to be selfish sometimes." Her smile wobbled, and then steadied. "You are a prince, after all."

"And yet it's not gaining me any ground with you, is it?"

She shook her head. "I'll come to the twins' birthday party."

It wasn't what she'd intended to say, but her heart had a mind of its own. Knowing she would never be able to take it back, Olivia remained silent as Gabriel escorted her to the waiting car and handed her into the backseat.

As the car rolled down the driveway, Olivia knew she'd been a fool to come here today. Obviously she hadn't learned anything these past few weeks. Gabriel held a power over her that was nothing short of dangerous. Thank goodness he would never know how unhappy she was without him because she had a feeling he might do something incredibly foolish.

Twelve

For the next two days leading up to his daughters' birthday party, Gabriel worked tirelessly to bring Christian up to speed on all the things that might come up in the next two weeks. After his last encounter with Olivia, he'd decided to take himself off the grid for a short time. Olivia's stubborn refusal to continue their relationship had forced Gabriel into a difficult position. Sherdana needed a royal heir. He needed Olivia. The opposing forces were tearing him apart.

On the morning of Bethany and Karina's birthday, Gabriel put his signature on the last report requiring his approval and went to have breakfast with his daughters. As usual they were full of energy and he smiled as he listened to their excited conversation.

It pleased him that Karina spoke more often now. Maybe she'd never be as talkative as her sibling, but as her confidence grew, she demonstrated a bright mind and a sly sense of humor. He had Olivia to thank for the transformation. She'd coaxed the younger twin out of her shell with patience and love. As attached as the trio had become, Gabriel was worried that Olivia's leaving would give rise to the girls' feelings of abandonment.

Scooping Karina onto his lap, he tickled her until she whooped with laughter. Could he make Olivia understand that there was more at stake than an heir for Sherdana?

Perhaps today's party would be the perfect opportunity to impress upon her how much she was needed and loved.

The festivities began at three. A large tent had been erected on the expansive lawn just east of the palace. A band played children's songs nearby and a dozen children jumped and twirled to the music in the open space between the stage and the linen-clad tables. Beyond that was a balloon bouncer shaped like a castle. The structure swayed as children burned off energy. On the opposite side of the lawn, their parents enjoyed more sedate entertainment in the form of an overflowing buffet of delicacies and free-flowing alcohol.

The crowd was a mix of wealthy nobility and leading businessmen. Gabriel stayed close to Bethany and Karina as they ate cake and played with the other children, keeping an eye out for Olivia as the afternoon progressed. She didn't arrive until almost five.

Looking pale and very beautiful in a light pink dress with short fluttery sleeves, she moved through the crowd, smiling politely when she encountered someone familiar, but otherwise avoiding eye contact with the guests.

Gabriel snagged a pair of wineglasses off the tray of a passing waiter. It was a chardonnay from one of Sherdana's finest wineries and he remembered how Olivia had wanted to tour the wine country. He added that to the list of things he'd promised and never delivered.

She caught sight of him when she was thirty feet away and very much looked as if she'd like to run away. Besieged by the memory of the kiss they'd shared in the nursery and the longing he'd tasted on her lips, Gabriel knew the only way to circumvent her stubbornness was to demonstrate the power of their passion for each other.

"I'm glad you came," he told her, as he drew close enough to speak. "I was beginning to worry that you wouldn't."

"I almost didn't." Her expression was rueful as she accepted the glass of wine he offered. "But I promised that I would."

"Bethany and Karina will be very glad."

Her gaze moved to where the twins were running with several children close to their age. "They look like they're having fun."

"All thanks to you. The party is fantastic."

"Libby did most of the work."

"But you are the one who came up with the concept and organized everything. You have quite a knack for party planning."

"In London I was on committees for several charities. I've done several large events, including children's parties. And speaking of children, I should probably say hello to Bethany and Karina. I won't be able to stay at the party long."

He inspected her face. Shadows beneath her eyes gave her the appearance of fragility. "Are you in pain?"

"Just tired." Her wan smile held none of her former liveliness. "My strength is not coming back as quickly as I'd like and I'm not sleeping well."

Gabriel tucked her hand into the crook of his arm and led her on a slow, meandering journey toward the twins, extending the amount of his time in her company. The tension in her slim frame troubled him and Gabriel wished he could do something to bring back the happy, vital woman she'd been two weeks earlier. He'd never felt so helpless.

Before he could bring her to where the twins were holding court, his daughters saw them coming and ran over. As they threw their tiny arms around her, Olivia's smile grew radiant. But there was sadness, as well. Sadness Gabriel knew he could banish if only she'd let him.

Hyped up on sweets and attention, the twins didn't linger long. After they'd raced back toward the other children, Olivia sidestepped away from Gabriel.

"I've taken up enough of your time," she said. "You have guests to attend to and I need to go."

He caught her wrist, preventing her from departing. "You're the only one I care about."

"Please don't," she pleaded in a hoarse whisper. "This is already so hard."

"And that's my fault." This wasn't a discussion he wanted to have in the middle of his daughters' birthday party, but he had to try one last time to reason with her. "Let me at least walk you out."

She must have seen his determination because she nodded.

Instead of leading her around the palace, he drew her through the doors leading to the green salon where they could have a little privacy.

"I'm sorry I didn't handle things better between us."

When he stopped in the middle of the room and turned her to face him she sighed. Looking resigned, she met his gaze. "You handled everything the way a future king should. I was the one who was wrong. I should have told you about my past medical issues before you had a chance to propose."

"What if I told you it wouldn't have mattered?" Gabriel lifted her hand and placed her palm over his heart.

"Then I would have to insult the crown prince of Sherdana by telling him he's a fool." She tried to pull her hand free, but he'd trapped it beneath his. Her tone grew more impatient. "You need an heir. That's something I can't give you."

"Unfortunate, yes. But that doesn't change the fact that I chose you and I'd committed to building a life with you. I'm not ready to give that up."

"That's madness," she exclaimed. "You have to. You must marry someone who can give you children."

Gabriel scowled at her response. "That's what the country needs me to do. But I'm not a country. I'm a man. A man who is tired of making everyone else's priorities his own."

"You don't have a choice," she whispered, blinking rapidly. "You are going to be king. You must do what's right. And so must I." With surprising strength, she wrenched her hand free and turned to flee.

"Olivia." He started after her, but realized nothing he could say at that moment would persuade her to change her mind.

Releasing a string of curses, Gabriel pulled out his cell phone and dialed. When the call connected, he said, "She won't budge."

"I'm sorry to hear that, Your Highness. The arrangements you asked for are complete and awaiting your arrival. Are you still planning on traveling the day after tomorrow?"

"Yes."

With the upheaval of the past several weeks, this was probably not the best time for him to leave the country, but he'd let the impossible situation with Olivia go on too long. She'd been right to say he didn't have a choice about his future. Fate had set him on a path and he needed to follow it to the end.

He found his parents together in the garden. They were strolling arm in arm, pausing here and there to greet their guests and enjoying the warm afternoon. He almost hated to spoil their peaceful moment.

"It was lovely of Olivia to come today," his mother said.

"She wanted to wish Bethany and Karina a happy birthday."

"You spent a lot of time with her." The queen's voice held a question.

Gabriel wondered how much his mother knew about his intentions. "It was her first social appearance since our engagement ended. I thought she could use the support."

"Of course. What happened with her was tragic and we cannot be seen turning our backs on her." Although the queen had spoken sympathetically about Olivia's plight, her priorities were her family and the country. "But you must not encourage her."

A bitter laugh escaped him. "She's well aware that I need a wife who can have children. If you think anything different, you don't appreciate her character."

The queen gave Gabriel a hard look. "Of course."

Gabriel shifted his gaze to his daughters. A trio of pre-teen girls were chasing the twins through the gardens. They laughed as they ran and Gabriel's heart lightened at the sound.

"I wanted to let you know," he began, returning his attention to his parents, "that in a couple days, I'm going out of town for a week or so."

"Is this the best time?" his father asked, echoing what Gabriel had been thinking minutes earlier.

"Perhaps not, but I have the future to think about and Sherdana still needs a princess."

The king frowned. "What about the state dinner for the Spanish ambassador?"

"Christian can take over while I'm gone." Gabriel forced his shoulders to relax. "I'm not the only prince in this family, you know. It's about time my brothers remembered that."

"I'm glad to hear you're ready to move forward," his mother said. "Can you give us some hint of your plans?"

"I'd rather wait until everything is finalized before I say anything."

"Very sensible," his father said and Gabriel wondered if the king would feel that way if he had any idea where his son was going and why.

Two days after the twins' birthday party, Olivia sat in an examination room, awaiting the doctor and fighting sadness. She was flying back to London in the morning. Back to her flat and her friends.

Her return would be far from triumphant. She'd been stripped of the ability to have children and because of that lost the man she loved. Thinking about the future only intensified her grief, so she'd spent the past few days finishing up the tasks she'd left undone such as the finalization of the menu for the hospital's children's wing gala taking place the following month and writing to cancel the invitations she'd accepted when she was still Gabriel's fiancée.

After ten minutes of waiting, Dr. Warner entered the room and interrupted her thoughts. Olivia was glad he accepted her assurances that she was getting along just fine in the wake of her hysterectomy and didn't voice the concern hovering in his expression. If he'd encouraged her to talk about her emotional health she might have burst into tears.

"Everything looks good," the doctor announced. "No reason you can't travel whenever you want."

"I'm leaving tomorrow," she said.

"Make sure you check in with your regular doctor within a week or two. He should be able to assist you with any side effects from your procedure and recommend a fertility specialist."

"Fertility specialist?" she echoed. "I don't understand. I can't have children."

"You can't bear children," the doctor agreed. "But your ovaries are intact. It might be possible to harvest your eggs and freeze them in case you decide to pursue motherhood in the future."

"I could be a mother?" Olivia breathed, overcome by the possibility that something she'd longed for with all her heart could still come to pass.

"You'd need to find a surrogate," the doctor said, his eyes twinkling. "And of course, you'd need a father, but it's certainly a possibility."

"I never imagined…" Her voice trailed off.

"Medical science is making miracles happen every day."

The doctor left her alone to dress and Olivia went through the motions in a daze. Her first impulse was to call Gabriel and tell him her news. Then she imagined how that call would go.

Gabriel, I have great news, I might be able to be a mother, after all. It's chancy and it will involve another woman carrying the baby, but it would be my egg.

Could a country as traditional as Sherdana accept a prince conceived in a test tube? And raised by a mother who hadn't actually carried him inside her for nine months?

Could Gabriel?

When Olivia returned to her suite at the hotel, she couldn't stop pacing as her mind spun through her options. Possible scenarios crowded her like desperate beggars in need of coin. Staring out the window at the river, she held her phone against her chest and searched for the courage she needed to dial Gabriel's number and tell him that she loved him and find out if he was willing to take a risk with her.

The sun had set by the time she dialed. With her heart pounding against her ribs, she counted rings, her hope fading as the number grew larger. When his deep voice poured through the receiver, telling her he was unavailable and asking her to leave a message at the tone, she held her breath for five seconds, then disconnected the call. She really didn't want to share her news with his voice mail.

Next, she tried Stewart. This time, she got through.

"I was trying to get ahold of Gabriel," she told his private secretary. "Do you know if he's in the palace?"

"No. He left two hours ago."

"Do you know where he went?" A long pause followed her question. Olivia refused to be put off by Stewart's reluctance. "It's important that I speak with him."

"I'm sorry, Lady Darcy. He has left the country."

"Did he go to Italy?"

Stewart paused before replying. "All he would tell me is that he had something he needed to do that would impact the future generations of Alessandros."

Olivia's stomach plummeted as she pictured Count Verreos and his beautiful daughter from the twins' birthday party and recalled the familiarity between her and Gabriel. Had they reached an understanding already? Was she Olivia's replacement?

"Is there any way to reach him?" she asked, desperation growing as she suspected where Gabriel and gone and why.

"I've left him several messages that he hasn't returned," Stewart answered, sounding unhappy.

"How long was he planning to be gone?"

"A week to ten days. Before departing, he left instructions that you should be given use of the royal family plane. It will be available to take you back to England tomorrow."

"That's kind of him." Although disappointed that Gabriel had at long last accepted their relationship was over, Olivia wasn't deterred. "But when you speak with him, would you tell him I intend to stay in Sherdana until we can speak face-to-face."

She hadn't believed Gabriel when he'd insisted this wasn't over between them. If only she'd known how right he was a couple days earlier.

After hanging up with Stewart, Olivia called her father and gave him the news that she was staying another week, but didn't share the real reason. To her relief, he didn't try to talk her into coming home immediately.

With nothing to do but wait, Olivia had an early dinner and took a walk in the private walled garden behind the hotel. Instead of enjoying the picturesque charm of the boxwood hedges and urns filled with cascades of bright flowers, Olivia grew more anxious with every step. What if Gabriel was proposing to Fabrizia Verreos at this very moment? A painful spasm in her chest forced Olivia to stop. Gasping for air, she sat down on a nearby stone bench and fought to normalize her breathing. She focused on the fat blossoms on the peach rosebush across the path from her. Closing her eyes would have allowed her mind to fill with images of another woman in Gabriel's arms.

A vibration against her upper thigh provided a welcome distraction. Pulling out her cell phone Olivia saw Stewart was calling. Her pulse hitched as hope bloomed.

"Prince Gabriel called me a few minutes ago," Stewart explained. "He is unable to return to Sherdana at the moment, but when I explained you intended to linger until he came home, he asked if you would fly to meet with him tomorrow."

It was what she wanted, but based on her panic attack a moment earlier, she was thinking that perhaps Gabriel intended to tell her in person that he was moving on.

"Of course." Afterward she could fly home.

"The plane will be waiting for you at ten. I'll send a car to pick you up."

"Thank you."

Olivia hung up and continued her walk, plagued by worries.

What if she didn't reach him before he proposed to Fabrizia? What if despite the passionate kiss he'd given her the day of the twins' birthday he wasn't willing to risk the unconventional method needed in order for them to conceive the next generation of Alessandros?

Pushing everything out of her mind that she couldn't control, Olivia concentrated on what she was going to say to Gabriel about the change in her circumstances. By the time Olivia returned to her room, she'd rehearsed and discarded a dozen ways to convince Gabriel they could have children. In the end, she decided the best argument was to tell him she loved him. And she was grateful she only had to wait hours instead of days before she could speak the truth of her heart.

The next morning saw her staring out the window with blurry vision as the royal family's private plane taxied down the runway. Plagued by uncertainty, she hadn't slept but an hour or so. Lulled by the drone of the engines, she shut her eyes and didn't realize she'd drifted off until the change in altitude woke her. Glancing at her watch, she saw that she'd been asleep for nearly two hours.

Stretching, she glanced out the window, expecting to see Italy's lush green landscape, but what greeted her eyes was shimmering blue water. The plane touched down smoothly and rolled toward a series of private hangers.

"Where are we?" she asked the copilot as he lowered the steps that would allow her to disembark into the foreign landscape.

"Cephalonia," the pilot answered, carrying her overnight bag down the steps to a waiting car. He handed her bag to the driver. "Greece."

"Thank you," she murmured to both men as she slid into the car's backseat. Although why she was thanking them, she had no idea. If they were kidnapping her, this was the oddest way to go about it.

"Where are we going?" she questioned the driver as he

navigated along a coastal road cut into the mountainside with a stunning view of the sea.

"Fiskardo."

Which told her absolutely nothing. The only thing she was certain of at this moment was that she was nowhere near Italy and Gabriel. What sort of trick had Stewart played on her? Was this some sort of plot to get her out of the way while Gabriel did his duty and secured himself a new fiancée?

If that was the case, Stewart better be the villain. If Gabriel had orchestrated this stunt, she was going to be even more heartbroken. Pulling out her phone, she dialed first Gabriel, then Stewart when the former still didn't answer. She had no luck getting through.

As soon as she arrived at her destination, she would figure out her next step. If this was Stewart's gambit, she would find another way to get in contact with Gabriel. Perhaps the queen would help.

With nothing to do for the moment, Olivia stared out the window as the car descended from the mountains and drove down into a seaside town. She'd never visited any of the Greek Ionian Islands before and acknowledged the scenery in this area was spectacular. At least Stewart had been kind enough to find a gorgeous place to squirrel her away. As the car navigated through town, she glimpsed the whitewashed houses with their flower-draped balconies and wondered if her final destination was one of the lovely hotels overlooking the harbor. Her spirits sank as they passed each one and came to a stop a short distance from the waterfront.

They were met by a handsome swarthy Greek in his midfifties who flashed blinding white teeth in a mischievous grin. Seeing his good humor restored her own. She followed him along the cement quay, lined with chartered sailboats, believing that there had to be a happy ending to all this adventuring.

"I am Thasos," he said as he helped her onto a luxurious thirty-four-foot cruiser.

"Where are we going, Thasos?" she questioned, accepting the glass of wine offered, glad for it and the tray of Greek food that awaited her.

"Kioni."

Another name that rang no bells. With a sigh, Olivia munched on bread, dolmas, cheese and olives while the boat sped out of the harbor. If she'd thought the water had appeared beautiful from the coast, it was nothing compared to the sparkling blue that surrounded her now. A short distance away, another island loomed, a great green hulk adorned with olive trees and cypress. Few houses dotted the mountainsides. She would have worried about being in such a remote area, but the bustle of the town they'd just left behind told her she hadn't been brought to the ends of the earth.

After polishing off a second glass of wine and taking the edge off her hunger, she stared at the coastline as it passed. Ninety minutes on the water brought them to another harbor, this one shaped like a horseshoe with three windmills on one side of its mouth.

"Kioni," Thasos explained with another wide grin.

Olivia sighed, wondering who was going to meet her here. Could she expect another taxi ride? Perhaps the plan was to keep her moving until she cried uncle. While Thasos maneuvered the boat toward the cement seawall that circled the harbor, Olivia gazed at this town. Smaller and less busy than Fiskardo, it nevertheless had the same charm. A few houses clustered close to the waterfront, but most clung to the side of the mountain that rose above this scenic harbor.

Everywhere she looked vivid purple and magenta bougainvillea vines brightened the whitewashed buildings or arched over the steps that led to the homes perched on the hillside. Silence descended as Thasos killed the motor and the light breeze brought the clank of cowbells to her ears. But she doubted the steep terrain was suitable for cows. More likely the bells she heard belonged to goats.

She stepped off the boat, helped by Thasos and another man, who claimed her bag for the next part of her journey. Olivia followed him for about thirty steps before she spied a tall, familiar figure coming down the street toward her.

Gabriel.

His white pants, pale blue shirt and navy blazer gave him the look of casual elegance. Her heart jumped in her chest as the wind tousled his hair. He slid his sunglasses up on his head as he approached and gave her a gentle smile.

He wasn't in Italy proposing to the daughter of an Italian count. He was here and from the expression on his face, he was very glad to see her.

Thirteen

The unguarded expression on Olivia's face when she spotted him made Gabriel the happiest man on earth. He was her white knight come to rescue her from the dragons. The fact that he was towing a donkey instead of a black charger hadn't made an impact on her yet.

"What are you doing here?" she demanded. "You're supposed to be in Italy."

He shook his head. "Italy? Where did you get that idea?"

"Stewart said you had gone to do something that would impact future generations of Alessandros. I assumed you meant to…propose to the daughter of Count Verreos." She touched the corner of her eye where a trace of moisture had gathered and a ragged exhale escaped her.

"No. I came straight here."

"Does Stewart know where you are?"

"No. I knew he wouldn't approve of what I intended to do."

"That's why I don't understand what are you doing here and why you dragged me all the way to Greece by plane, across an island by car and now here by boat."

"I needed some time to prepare." He grinned. "And I thought you might be less likely to argue with me if you were tired."

"Argue about what?" she demanded, her gaze drawn

toward the small donkey that stood beside him, ears flickering lazily forward and back. "And what are you doing with that?"

Gabriel patted the donkey's neck. "It's traditional for Greek brides to ride donkeys to their weddings."

"Bride? What are you talking about...?" Her voice trailed off as she noticed the donkey came equipped with a riding pad covered with flowers. "You can't be serious."

She sounded aghast, but hope glowed in her blue eyes.

"I'm utterly serious. The church and the priest are waiting for us. All you need to do is hop on." Seeing she wasn't fully on board with his plan, he caught her around the waist and pulled her body flush with his, taking care to treat her gently. "Marry me." He drew his knuckles down her cheek. "Please. I can't live without you."

Tears flooded her eyes. "You love me?"

"I love you. I adore you. You're my world." He peered down at her in surprise. "Haven't you figured that out by now?"

She took his hand and drew it away from her skin. Her grip was tight enough to make him wince.

"What of your parents' wishes? Have you considered the barrage of negative opinions you'll face when we return home?"

"None of that matters. No one matters but us. I have two brothers, both of whom are capable of getting married and having children. There's no reason why I have to be the one who fathers the next generation of Sherdana royalty. It was different when my father became king. He was the only direct male descendant. And besides, I think it's time my brothers took on a little royal responsibility."

A crowd of townspeople and tourists were gathering on the narrow street, drawn by the novelty of a decked out donkey and the argument between Gabriel and Olivia. The late-afternoon sun bathed the town in golden light, softening the scenery. The breeze off the harbor was gentle against Olivia's skin, soothing her anxiety.

"Neither one of them is going to be happy."

"I don't care. It's my turn to be a little selfish. We're getting married. Now. Today. And I'm not taking no for an answer."

That he was ready to marry her despite her inability to give him children thrilled her, and she could no longer wait to share her news.

"There's something I need to tell you."

"That you love me?"

"No."

"You don't?" he teased.

"Of course I do. But that's not what I need to tell you."

"But don't you think it's an appropriate thing to tell your groom on your wedding day?"

"Very well. I love you."

"When you say it like that, I'm not sure I believe you."

She leaned forward and slid her fingers into his hair, drawing him close for a slow, deep kiss. "I love you."

His response was almost a purr. "Much better."

"Now are you ready to hear what I have to say?"

"Yes."

Their impending nuptials had certainly brought out the mischief maker in Gabriel. Or perhaps it was getting away from the palace and all his responsibility. Olivia made a note to kidnap him at least once a year and bring him somewhere with no cell phones and no television so they could get reacquainted.

"When I spoke with the doctor yesterday—" she gathered a deep breath "—he gave me some rather startling news."

The wicked light died in Gabriel's eyes. He grew somber. He caught her fingers in a tight grip. "Is something wrong?"

"No. In fact, I think everything might be okay in time."

"How so?"

"He thinks that a fertility specialist might be able to harvest eggs from my ovaries." She watched Gabriel carefully, hoping he was open to what she had in mind. "It would require finding a woman willing to be a surrogate, but it's possible that you and I could still make babies together."

"This is the most amazing news."

Gabriel caught her around the waist and pulled her against his body. Dipping his head, he captured her lips with his for a long, slow kiss.

By the time he released her mouth they were both breathing heavily. Gabriel's eyes sparkled like the sun on the water behind them. Joy sped through her as she realized she was about to marry the man she adored.

"Come on, let's get you up on the donkey and get to the church."

"Are you sure it's tradition?" she protested, eyeing the creature doubtfully.

"Positive."

Their parade up the steep street to the church was not the formal affair it would have been in Sherdana. There was no gilded carriage pulled by six perfectly matched white horses. No thousands of people lining the streets to wave and throw rose petals at them. But there were smiles and hearty cheers as Gabriel lead the donkey through the heart of the town.

When they reached the church, Gabriel introduced his housekeeper, Elena, who took Olivia aside to help her into the modest knee-length wedding dress with cap sleeves and a large bow at the waist. A note from Noelle accompanied the dress, explaining that Libby had come to her a few days after Olivia went into the hospital because Gabriel was planning on marrying Olivia in a small island wedding and wanted a dress to suit the occasion.

So, despite his lack of contact during her hospital stay, Gabriel hadn't accepted that their engagement was at an end. He'd still wanted her as his wife, even though his family and political advisers would counsel him to move on.

Awash with joy, Olivia clutched the note to her chest and stared at her reflection. Although the design was much simpler than the lace-and-crystal-embellished gown she'd have worn to marry Gabriel in Sherdana, it was perfect. As was the man who awaited her at the front of the beautiful Greek church.

Gabriel's gaze never once wavered as she walked toward him, accompanied by the song of a single violin. There was no doubt, no restraint in his golden eyes, only possessiveness, and she reveled in his love.

He took her hand as she came to stand beside him and she tingled in delight. Elena and her husband were the only witnesses. The intimacy of the empty church allowed them the privacy to focus completely on each other and they exchanged vows in reverent tones. When they returned to Sherdana, there would be celebrations with family and friends. Until then, all they wanted was each other.

After the ceremony, they exited the church and encountered a small crowd. Apparently Gabriel and his brothers were well liked in the coastal town and when word got out that he had come to the island to get married, many had turned out to wish him and Olivia well.

They lingered for several minutes, greeting people and accepting congratulations until Gabriel insisted it was time he took his bride home. Laughing and shaking his head at good-natured invitations to stay in town and celebrate their wedding, Gabriel slipped his arm around her waist and began to edge out of the circle of people.

"My car is this way." He took her hand and began to lead her down the road.

"Oh, thank goodness, I was afraid you'd make me ride the donkey back to your house."

Gabriel laughed heartily. "It would take him too long to carry you that far and I can't wait that long to have you all to myself."

Once he got her settled in the passenger seat and slid behind the wheel, he sat sideways in his seat and regarded her intently.

After several seconds of his attentive silence, Olivia grew restless. "What are you doing?"

"Appreciating our first private moment as husband and wife. The circumstances of the last few weeks haven't given us any time together and when we leave here, there will be public appearances and meetings demanding our time. I intend to spend every possible moment until then showing my beautiful wife how much I adore her."

Being his wife was her dream come true. Olivia smiled. "If I'm beautiful, you have Noelle to thank for that." She gestured to her wedding dress. "Have you really been planning this romantic elopement since before I left the hospital?"

"It was your secretary's idea. She knows how stubborn you can be and came to me with a crazy plan that I should steal you away to someplace exotic and marry you."

"Libby?" Olivia considered her secretary's encouragement anytime Olivia had doubted her future with Gabriel.

"She helped me with the dress and arranged the church and the flowers."

"How were you planning to get me to agree to run off with you?"

"By offering you a ride home in our jet and then bringing you here. You made things a lot easier by asking to see me."

"Did Stewart have any idea what you were planning?"

Gabriel shook his head. "Stewart's loyalty is to Sherdana. Libby's loyalty is to you." He leaned forward and pressed a lingering kiss on her lips. "And so is mine."

Olivia contemplated her new husband during the short drive to his villa, a two-mile journey around the horseshoe-shaped harbor. Never again would she underestimate his determination or his loyalty to her. He'd been willing to go against his family for her. She couldn't ask for a better partner or soul mate.

Because they'd been delayed in town Elena had already arrived and was in the process of arranging a romantic table for them on the terrace high above the harbor. At Olivia's prompting, Gabriel gave her a brief tour of the villa. In the spacious bedroom they would share, Gabriel drew her toward the window and they stared out at Kioni, its lights glowing bright as dusk descended. With his arms wrapped around Olivia's waist and his chin resting on her head, he sighed.

Olivia chuckled. "Was that weariness or contentment?"

"Contentment. You will be hearing many more such sighs in the coming days while we enjoy some much-needed privacy."

"We will have to go back eventually."

His arms tightened around her. "I prefer not to think about that moment until it arrives."

"Won't the media come here looking for us?"

"In the past we've kept a low profile and the people who live on the island respect our privacy." His lips trailed of fire down her neck. "Now, let's go downstairs and enjoy our first dinner as man and wife."

They returned to the first floor and accepted glasses of champagne from Elena. She gestured them out onto the terrace and retreated to fetch the first course.

"This is beautiful," Olivia commented, admiring the simple but elegant scene.

With the sunset long past, the sky had deepened to indigo. A row of white candles stretched along the low terrace wall, pushing back the darkness, their flames protected by glass containers. More candles had been placed in the center of the table, their flickering glow making shadows dance over the fine white tablecloth, beautiful china and colorful flower arrangements.

Gabriel led her to the table and helped her into a linen-clad chair before taking his own seat beside her. The romantic lighting softened his strong bone structure and brought out the sensual curve of his lips as he smiled. "Here's to following our hearts."

Olivia smiled as she clinked her glass to his and marveled at her good fortune. She never would have guessed that she had to lose everything in order to gain the one thing she needed most.

Setting her glass down, Olivia reached for Gabriel's hand.

"A few weeks ago your sister told me to ask you something. I never did."

"Ask now."

"She said we'd met before six months ago. Is that true?"

"Yes."

"But I don't recall meeting you. And I assure you I would. Were we young children? Is that why I don't remember?"

"It was almost seven years ago at a masquerade party. Given the host's reputation I was a little surprised to discover the young woman I rescued was none other than Lady Olivia Darcy."

Gabriel had been her savior. The man whose kiss had set the bar for every other romantic encounter she'd had since. "You knew who I was?"

"Not until after you'd left and Christian informed me who I'd been kissing." Gabriel's fingertips grazed her cheek. "When I kissed you that night, something sparked between us. I wasn't ready to get married and you were far too young, but something told me you were the woman I was destined to marry."

"But that was one kiss seven years ago." She couldn't imagine how a single moment in time could impact him so strongly. And yet hadn't she felt the magic between them? Compared his kiss to those that came after? "And my father approached you about building a plant in Sherdana."

"That's true, but Christian put the idea in his head. My brother is very clever when it comes to business dealings and had an inkling of how much you interested me."

"But you loved Marissa. You would have married her if Sherdanian law had allowed it."

"I never wanted to marry Marissa. She was my way of rebelling against duty and responsibility. I loved being with her, but I know now that I didn't love her. Not the way I love you."

His lips found hers and delivered a kiss that managed to be both incredibly arousing and spiritually satisfying at the same time. Olivia was weak with delight when he set her free.

"I can't quite believe all that has happened today," she murmured as his fingertips worked their way along her shoulder. "When I woke up this morning I was cautiously optimistic. Now I'm happier than I ever imagined I could be."

Gabriel gifted her with a smile of resolute tenderness. "And it's my intention to do whatever it takes to ensure you stay that way."

After disappearing from the radar for a week, and then reappearing with a glowing bride in tow, Gabriel had anticipated a media frenzy, but he hadn't expected the capital's streets to be lined with people.

In the back of the limousine, Olivia waved at the enthusiastic crowd, looking every inch a princess. But by the time the vehicle pulled up in front of the palace, her nerves had begun to show.

"Are we going to be taken to the gallows and shot?" she questioned. "Is that why everyone turned out to see us?"

"A member of Sherdana's royal family hasn't been executed in almost three hundred years."

"That's not as reassuring as you want it to be."

Gabriel squeezed her hand. "Everything is going to be fine."

"Since when are you such an optimist?"

"Since marrying you."

A footman stepped forward to open the limo's door. Olivia nodded toward a glowering Christian, who was striding through the palace's ornate main doors.

"He doesn't look happy."

"I think he's realized the trap has been sprung."

"You sound as if you're enjoying this far too much."

"Do you have any idea how many dossiers I looked through over the years, weighing my future happiness against what was right for the country, while my brothers ran around the United States and Europe following their dreams?"

"A hundred?" she offered.

"Try a thousand."

"Surely there weren't that many girls who wanted to marry you," she teased.

"Oh, there were at least three times that, but only one girl I wanted to marry."

"You really have become a smooth talker. No wonder I fell in love with you."

Christian extended a hand to assist Olivia as she exited the car and kissed her on each cheek before glowering at Gabriel over a perfunctory handshake.

"How are things?" Gabriel asked, overlooking his brother's surly mood. He kept ahold of Olivia's hand as they made their way into the palace.

"Sherdana's been doing just fine," Christian muttered.

"I meant with you. Has Mother come up with a list of potential candidates for your bride yet?"

"You really are a bastard."

"Don't let our mother hear you say that." He thumped his brother on the back. "But what do you have to worry about? Nic is next in line. The burden to produce an heir falls on him first."

"Mother's not taking any chances this time. She thinks both of us should be married."

"I agree with her. Nothing like marrying the woman of your dreams to know complete and perfect happiness."

Gabriel laughed heartily at Christian's look of disgust and followed Olivia up the stairs. As they entered the suite of rooms she and Gabriel would now be sharing, she leaned close and spoke in a low voice. "Why didn't you tell Christian there's a potential we can have children?"

He shut the door to the suite, ensuring their privacy, and took her in his arms. "I think we should keep this development our little secret for the time being."

"Are you sure?" Olivia reached up and threaded her

fingers through Gabriel's dark hair. "If it works, it will let your brothers off the hook."

"There's no reason to say anything until we have something definitive to tell."

"That could take months," she exclaimed, her eyes wide with uncertainty. "They could be engaged or even married by then."

"Making you my wife has been the best thing that could have happened to me. I think my brothers deserve to experience the same."

"You're going to force them into a situation where they have to find wives so that they'll fall in love?"

"Diabolical, isn't it?"

"They'll kill you when they find out the truth."

"I don't think so." Gabriel leaned down and silenced further protests with a deep, soul-stirring kiss. "I think they'll thank me for making them the second and third happiest men on the planet."

"You being the first?" She arched her eyebrows at him.

Gabriel responded with a broad grin. "Absolutely."

* * * * *

REQUEST YOUR FREE BOOKS!
2 FREE NOVELS PLUS 2 FREE GIFTS!

⬦HARLEQUIN®

Desire

ALWAYS POWERFUL, PASSIONATE AND PROVOCATIVE

YES! Please send me 2 FREE Harlequin Desire® novels and my 2 FREE gifts (gifts are worth about $10). After receiving them, if I don't wish to receive any more books, I can return the shipping statement marked "cancel." If I don't cancel, I will receive 6 brand-new novels every month and be billed just $4.55 per book in the U.S. or $4.99 per book in Canada. That's a savings of at least 13% off the cover price! It's quite a bargain! Shipping and handling is just 50¢ per book in the U.S. and 75¢ per book in Canada.* I understand that accepting the 2 free books and gifts places me under no obligation to buy anything. I can always return a shipment and cancel at any time. Even if I never buy another book, the two free books and gifts are mine to keep forever.

225/326 HDN F4ZC

Name _____ (PLEASE PRINT) _____

Address _____ Apt. #

City _____ State/Prov. _____ Zip/Postal Code

Signature (if under 18, a parent or guardian must sign)

Mail to the **Harlequin® Reader Service:**
IN U.S.A.: P.O. Box 1867, Buffalo, NY 14240-1867
IN CANADA: P.O. Box 609, Fort Erie, Ontario L2A 5X3

Want to try two free books from another line?
Call 1-800-873-8635 or visit www.ReaderService.com.

* Terms and prices subject to change without notice. Prices do not include applicable taxes. Sales tax applicable in N.Y. Canadian residents will be charged applicable taxes. Offer not valid in Quebec. This offer is limited to one order per household. Not valid for current subscribers to Harlequin Desire books. All orders subject to credit approval. Credit or debit balances in a customer's account(s) may be offset by any other outstanding balance owed by or to the customer. Please allow 4 to 6 weeks for delivery. Offer available while quantities last.

Your Privacy—The Harlequin® Reader Service is committed to protecting your privacy. Our Privacy Policy is available online at www.ReaderService.com or upon request from the Harlequin Reader Service.

We make a portion of our mailing list available to reputable third parties that offer products we believe may interest you. If you prefer that we not exchange your name with third parties, or if you wish to clarify or modify your communication preferences, please visit us at www.ReaderService.com/consumerschoice or write to us at Harlequin Reader Service Preference Service, P.O. Box 9062, Buffalo, NY 14269. Include your complete name and address.

HD13R